IN REPAIR

IN REPAIR

A.L. Graziadei

GODWIN BOOKS
HENRY HOLT AND COMPANY
NEW YORK

Henry Holt and Company, *Publishers since 1866*
Henry Holt® is a registered trademark of Macmillan Publishing Group, LLC
120 Broadway, New York, NY 10271 • fiercereads.com

Our books may be purchased in bulk for promotional, educational, or business use.
Please contact your local bookseller or the Macmillan Corporate and
Premium Sales Department at (800) 221-7945 ext. 5442 or by email at
MacmillanSpecialMarkets@macmillan.com.

Library of Congress Control Number: 2023046284

First edition, 2024
Book design by Maria W. Jenson
Printed in the United States of America

ISBN 978-1-250-77713-3
1 3 5 7 9 10 8 6 4 2

FOR ME, FOR LISA, AND THE KIDS WE WERE.

CONTENT WARNINGS:

Implied past CSA, past self-harm,
self-harm scars, dissociation, suicidal
ideation, referenced past child abuse,
referenced past suicide.

CHAPTER 1

I EXPECTED A SOFTER landing than this.

With the two seconds I took to scope the drop before jumping, I thought I'd be sinking into a snowy, pillowy shrub that I could roll off the top of and make my escape with ease.

But there's no snow built up along the foundation of the building, and bushes are apparently a lot stabbier than they look and very easy to crash through.

I keep my eyes closed and breathe softly through my mouth. It's freezing out here. My shirt was damp with sweat from that crowded double room, but now it's soaked with the melting snow that piled on top of me in the wake of my destruction.

There's warmth on my face, though. On my arm. Warmth and a familiar sting, like the branches fought back. I swipe my knuckles across my cheek and they come back bloodied.

"And what about the guy that went out the window? What's his name?"

The gruff voice of one of the campus safety officers drifts

down from above, and a smile stretches across my face. I wish I could pinpoint the exact moment the trajectory of my life shifted to lead me to this, lying in the snowy bushes outside a college dorm while the party I was at gets busted.

Maybe it was the first time I slipped a candy bar into my pocket at the grocery store, eyes on my mom, waiting for her to turn around and catch me in the act. She never did.

Or maybe it was the time I sat on the curb with my hands cuffed behind my back, red and blue lights burned so deeply into my retinas, I saw them every time I closed my eyes for days afterward.

Really, it was probably the moment my dad sat me in front of the family computer with tab after tab of college apps slowing the Wi-Fi to a crawl and said, "It's this or prison."

I'd mumbled, "You'd know all about that, wouldn't you?" and Dad snapped back with a "Yes. I would."

He watched me fill out every one of those apps, put in his bank information for the fee on each one, but still, I never thought I'd find myself here.

"I don't know—I think he's some freshman?" a guy in the room says. "Nathan or something? I didn't even invite him."

I scrub another bead of blood from my face.

I might not have been invited, but I was absolutely the life of that party, with everyone enraptured by my cardistry and storytelling.

"All right, one of you guys wanna go look for him while I

do this? Make sure he didn't break his neck," the officer says, and I push myself to my feet, scrambling out of the bushes and away from the building.

I brush snow and broken twigs off my clothes as I stagger down the hill toward the walkway. Shake out my hair. I angle away from the main exit around the corner of the building, letting my footprints in the snow make it look like I headed toward the center of campus before cutting back once I hit the shoveled, salted path. Campus safety won't expect me to walk right past them. I was out the window before the door fully opened, before they could get a good look at me, but I pull my hood up anyway. With my middle part and the black and white split dye job, it's best to cover up when I'm trying to avoid notice.

With a deep breath of icy midwinter air, I stretch my arms over my head, twisting at the waist to make sure I didn't really hurt myself. My tailbone feels a little sore, and there's that burn on my left arm that has me tugging down my sleeves. But when I wipe at my cheek again, no more blood comes away.

A couple people stand in the light of a streetlamp at the base of the dorm's main steps, looking right at me as I round the corner, like they were expecting me. Guess I made a bit of noise as I crashed through the bushes, no matter how gracefully I tried to fall. I slouch my shoulders and put on an easy grin as I head their way.

"Hello, hello," I say in a singsong, sliding my hands into the pockets of my shredded black jeans. I stop close enough to look like I'm with them without encroaching too much on their space.

"Did you just jump out a window?" the girl in black jeans and a purple puffer jacket asks me. She's absolutely in my public speaking class, but I've never talked to her before. Think her name is Celeste? She's Mexican, dark hair that hangs down to her waist, covered by a white beanie with a rose embroidered into the front.

"*Pfft*, what?" I say. "No."

"We literally watched you," says Celeste's friend. I don't recognize them, but they've got a *they/them* pin on their denim jacket, along with nonbinary and pansexual pride colored ghosts and a little witch hat. They're Korean, wearing a burgundy dress that looks like it's made of velvet over black tights. They hold their knees together like they're freezing. Their black hair is cut to their chin, half of it pulled into a tiny ponytail with bangs cut straight across their forehead. "We've been waiting to see who'd come around."

I cock my head to the side and smile with all my teeth. "Couldn't've been me."

They both give me unimpressed looks, and the door up the stairs behind them opens on one of the campus safety officers. He pulls a flashlight from his utility belt and jogs down the stairs, giving us a nod on his way by but barely looking at us. We watch him trudge through the snow up the hill, completely missing the footprints a few feet farther. He disappears around the corner.

"Y'know, if you were at a dorm party or something, you'd probably just get a warning," Celeste says. "Not a big deal. I mean, unless it's not the first time?"

I put a hand over my heart and scoff in mock offense. "I am extremely innocent."

"So you just get your kicks from jumping out of windows and running from campus safety for no reason?"

"Who's running?" I say with a shrug.

I'm practically begging her to pry. The more she pushes, the more I can push back, the more nonchalant I can appear, the more intriguing I can become.

It's not like I was afraid of a slap on the wrist from campus safety. I wasn't drinking at that party, so I had nothing to worry about. It's just that crashing parties and jumping out of windows gets people to talk about a person, and if there's one thing I want out of this life, it's for people to talk about me.

But Celeste doesn't pry any further. She narrows her eyes and purses her lips to the side, and her friend whose name I don't know snorts a laugh.

I let my hand fall from my chest. "I am feeling very judged right now."

Celeste raises both hands in a semblance of surrender

and shakes her head. "No judgment here. It's actually kind of hilarious. Nathaniel, right?"

It's a rush, having a practical stranger know my name. "That's me. And you're . . . Callie?"

Her eye roll is knowing. "Celeste Hernandez. This is Tasha Seo."

Tasha gives me a smile and a small wave, eyes sweeping over me from head to toe. There's a camera bag hanging from their shoulder. "I really love your look."

Another rush, being ogled like that. I dress like I do for that exact purpose. With my torn-up jeans and chain hanging from my belt, the short-sleeved hoodie and the striped long-sleeve tee underneath. The hair. The black nail polish. The dangling earrings and ear cuffs. The eye shadow under my eyes to make me look tired in an aesthetic kind of way.

Mom and Dad refused to buy me makeup and nail polish and flashy jewelry when I lived with them. I still managed to get my hands on it.

"How do you feel about modeling?" Tasha asks.

I try not to act surprised, like this is a question I get regularly, but I can't hide it from my voice. "Like, in general?"

"No, I'm—"

"Hey, you guys seen some drunk kid come through here?"

The three of us look back toward the window I came from, where the campus safety guy is plodding toward us.

He looks beyond bored, like he can't believe this is what his life has come to, searching for college kids in bushes. As he moves more into the light and gets a good look at me, there's a moment where I'm sure he's going to make the connection. But my clothes are dark enough to hide how damp they are, and Tasha is shivering just as violently as I am, and I probably seem way too unconcerned to be who he's looking for.

Plus, he's looking for *some drunk kid*, and I am 1,000 percent sober.

His lip curls as he takes in my appearance. I can practically hear his internal rant on generational trends.

I smile at him.

"No?" Celeste says, making a show of glancing around at the empty sidewalk. Shrieking laughter echoes from further into campus, and I crane my neck to get a glimpse of a group of people as they step into the main building.

The officer sighs, one hand on his hip and the other pinching the bridge of his nose. "You didn't hear anyone fall out a window?"

Tasha gives an impressively convincing wince. "Oh, that. Yeah, he went that way." They point over the officer's shoulder in the direction of my footprints. "He gave a thumbs-up when we asked if he was okay, though."

The officer shakes his head and grumbles to himself as he starts back up the stairs. "I'm not playing hide-and-seek." He gets halfway up before tossing over his shoulder at us, "Stay out of trouble!"

"Will do!" I call after him. We watch him leave, and as soon as the door closes behind him, I laugh. "Wow. Honestly, I didn't really think about it before going out the window. It was there and open, so I went for it. Surprised it worked."

"Surprised you didn't break your neck," Celeste deadpans.

I shrug her off. "The bushes broke my fall."

"Still."

My arms sting with the scratch of branches through my sleeves and there's blood on my knuckles, but I bite my tongue, press against the cut on my face with my fingertips, and keep on smiling.

"Seriously, though," Tasha says. "I'm looking for people to shoot for a photography project. Would you be interested?"

I stop myself from asking why they'd want me. Self-doubt doesn't fit the persona I'm trying to cultivate this semester.

"Yeah, I'd be down," I say. Casually. Completely unaffected.

They clap their hands in front of their chest and bounce on their toes. "Awesome! You have Insta?"

I spell out my Instagram name for them and get a follow notification a moment later. I follow them back and do a quick scroll through a profile filled with artsy—and really beautiful—photos.

"I'll message you the details when I have it all figured out," they say.

"Sounds good." I put my phone away and take out my deck of Star Wars–themed playing cards instead, sliding off the rubber bands as I pull them from my pocket. "You two have plans tonight?"

"We're actually late to some team bonding because of you," Celeste says. She glances at her phone. "Bailey's blowing up the group chat."

Tasha sighs heavily, brushing hair behind their ear. "Would hate to make the captain angry."

"See you in class Tuesday?" Celeste asks me.

"I'll be there."

She quirks an eyebrow. "If you don't fall out any more windows."

Tasha wiggles their fingers at me as they leave, heading toward the north road off campus.

As soon as their backs are turned, I deflate. My shoulders come forward as my head falls to the side. My body feels empty. Like I don't possess it unless I have eyes on me.

It takes teeth-gritting effort to get myself moving again, like the February cold has seeped into my bones, freezing my joints in place. I drag my feet back to my building, up the stairs to my floor, and the sound of laughter in the lounge shocks me back into my body.

I stand up straighter, plaster on a crooked smile, and dribble my deck of cards from hand to hand as I step into view of the lounge.

It's not until I have the attention of everyone in the room that I feel real again.

CHAPTER 2

Hartland University@hartlanduni-14hr
Students, first floor windows are higher than they appear. Please don't use them as exits, except in case of emergency.

I WASN'T ALWAYS LIKE this. Needing eyes on me the way I need oxygen in my blood.

In fact, it's a brand-new addiction.

I spent fall semester of my freshman year of college holed up in my dorm room, only emerging for classes, meals at the tail end of each time slot when the dining hall was at its emptiest. I didn't want to see people and I sure as hell didn't want them to see me.

I passed the semester unnoticed, and when I went home for winter break, I sat at the kitchen table while Mom and Dad asked about friends, campus events, anything noteworthy, anything at all . . . I had nothing to say.

College on its own had never been in my life plan. I was

meant to be a student-athlete, never just a student. Once lacrosse fell apart for me, I had no passion left for anything. At least not anything I was willing to put myself into inescapable debt over. But hearing my parents ask about the people, the campus life, not just grades and classes—which, don't get me wrong, they asked about plenty—made me realize that college doesn't have to be just a gateway into the workforce. I can use these years to remake myself and shape the way people see me.

My college education can be dedicated to creating the person I want to be.

And that person isn't afraid to leave their dorm room, or be seen, or talk to people. The ideal Nathaniel Conti doesn't care what people think of him and will do anything to prove it.

I can't spend my life locked inside my own head. I need to be seen.

And people sure see me now.

They do a double take as I walk past them Monday morning. Point me out to their friends. Laugh. There's a part of me—very small and tucked in the way back of my mind—that burns with embarrassment. It's the same part of me that remembers the way people looked at me in middle school, with my greasy hair and oily skin. My nose, too big for my face. My ill-fitting clothes courtesy of an older brother who's two inches shorter than me and far more muscly.

I shove that part of me—capable of feeling shame—even further down and choose to bask in the attention instead.

I've become something of a meme on the Hartland University corner of social media. This wild freshman who only seemed to spring into existence at the January return to campus. My dive out the window is all anyone's talked about all weekend. Someone referred to me as *that obnoxious e-boy*. Someone else dubbed me Cruella because of my hair.

It feels different than the baseless bullying of middle school. Now, they're entertained by me, and that's more than I could ask for.

I skip breakfast in the dining hall in favor of stopping by the campus café. I don't come here often, because I never have any money, but someone in my floor's lounge made the mistake of trusting the Honor Code and using a fully punched BUY 5, GET 1 FREE drink ticket as a bookmark. I snatched it when they left their book behind for a bathroom break.

The line is six people deep, most of them on their phones, some of them blinking off into space as they struggle to stay awake, fingers curled around their backpack straps. No one spares me a glance as I come in. I squint up at the chalkboard menu, the food and drink options interspersed with

Valentine's Day hearts and cupid's arrows, matching cutouts hanging from string like garland across the front counter.

I scratch at the thin scabs on my forearm, hidden under my sleeves. The branches might have done more damage than I thought at first. It's taken a lot of intentional thought diversion to not let it send me into a relapse. It was easier in the dining hall at peak meal hours. Sitting by myself in the Throne Room, surrounded by the sounds of laughter and conversation. Walking laps around campus just to be near people.

Alone in my room at night, with my roommate off hanging out with his girlfriend, it wasn't so easy anymore. That's when I had to tuck my hands into my sleeves, bunch the fabric in my fists, go to sleep just to shut off my brain for a little bit.

Now, I shove my hands in my pockets to stop scratching as I wait in line. Bite down on the inside of my cheek to brace against the barrage of thoughts. It's too quiet in here under the grinding of coffee beans, everyone too sleepy for eavesdroppable conversation. My head doesn't do well in quiet.

My name spoken behind me, a little to my right, almost startles me into oblivion. I take a moment to arrange my face into something less shocked before turning to look at Celeste.

"Celeste," I say, matching her matter-of-fact tone.

"I see you survived the rest of the weekend," she says.

"Skin of my teeth."

She looks me up and down and actually smiles, a crooked thing with her full lips pressed together. She's wearing rolled-cuff jeans and an oversized grandpa-looking sweater that swallows up her hands. She motions to her own face. "That eye shadow or do you never sleep?"

"The exhaustion is all-natural," I say. Might not answer her question exactly, but at least it's half the truth.

"You look like a haunted Victorian child. Like you've been forced to work the graveyard shift in a mineshaft for three months straight without a day off, and now you're dying of consumption."

"Thank you."

The bell above the exit chimes, drawing my eye as a guy I recognize from the public speaking class I share with Celeste ducks in, head down, face shadowed by his wind-blown brown curls. Well, I guess *duck* isn't exactly the right word for it. Mickey James's defining feature is his height. Or lack of it. I don't think he's ever had to duck under anything in his life.

Celeste and I both watch as he stalks over to us, stopping close enough that he has to lift his chin to glare up at her.

"I cannot believe you left me out there," he says in that gruff voice I've come to admire during his speeches in class. A stray curl falls into his eyes and he rakes it back with his fingers.

And all right, he might be short, but he has a deceptively

athletic build, with the way his jeans hug his thighs and the definition of his shoulders shows through his jacket. He and Celeste share a table across the room from me, so I've never gotten a good, up-close look at him. His face is red from the cold, expressionless, and slightly sunken. Like a recovering corpse.

"Aw, c'mon Terzo," Celeste says, overly sweet. "He seemed nice."

"He *seemed* like a creep trying to dig up all my dirty secrets."

She waves her hand dismissively, examining her dark red fingernails and their little pink glitter hearts for the holiday. "Such is the price of fame."

He narrows his eyes at her. "I'm not famous."

Now that he's done chastising Celeste, he finally turns to look at me. I meet his honey brown eyes, searching for what I missed. Maybe he's some kind of social media influencer? I could see him doing voice-over commentary on viral videos, with that dry tone of his. Oooh, or *maybe* he posts thirst traps, throwing people off with his stature and then hitting them with surprise muscles.

His lip curls after I stare too long and too intently. "What?"

I tilt my head to the side and make a show of leaning all my weight on one foot, ever casual. "I didn't realize you two were friends."

They might share a table in class, but I've only ever seen Celeste talk to the other guy that sits with them. They don't whisper to each other through the hour like the trio of friends who sit right in front of me. Mickey spends the whole class looking mildly pissed off, but now that I'm seeing him up close, I think that might just be his natural resting face.

Celeste puts a hand over her heart and takes a step back, screwing her face up at me. "We are definitely *not* friends."

Mickey rolls his eyes, but I catch a hint of a smile. "No, she's just spying on me for my sister."

She jabs a finger into the center of his chest. "Bailey strongly hinted that if I make sure you pass these classes, she'll put a good word in to Coach for next year."

"You are not going to be captain as a sophomore, Celeste, I'm sorry."

"What do you know about captaincy?"

They continue bickering as the barista calls me up to the counter and I hand over the drink ticket. She looks down at it, then up at me, and then at the name scrawled across the top. "You look different today, Corey."

I give her a breezy laugh. "Yeah, he said he wouldn't get to use it before it expires, so he let me have it."

"They don't expire."

"Oh. Huh." I shrug. "Maybe he was too shy to call it a Valentine's gift."

She raises one pierced eyebrow and gives me a look like she knows every word is utter bullshit. I put on my purest, most innocent smile, and after a moment, she rolls her eyes. "I don't even care. What do you want?"

I order a latte with extra espresso shots and step to the side as Celeste and Mickey take their turns, still arguing whenever they get the chance. I tug on my sleeves as I wait, making sure every bit of skin down to my fingertips is covered.

What if they finish ordering and don't come over to stand with me? What if they stop a few feet away, just the two of them, making it clear I'm not with them? Leaving me on my own.

I can already feel myself detaching at the edges. Like my mind wants to be as far from my body as it can get to avoid the inevitable rejection.

I read the menu board again and again. Clench my fists around the bunched fabric of my shirtsleeves and focus on the smell of coffee grounds and steamed milk. The low murmur of sleepy voices coming from the table behind me. The door chime as someone leaves and the bright, "Thanks!" when they hold the door for someone else.

Remind myself I am not alone. I am surrounded by people, and even if they aren't with me, they see me. I am still here.

"Oh, that's funny." Mickey's voice cuts through the fog

settling in my head, not a hint of humor despite his words. "You should tell that joke at the talent show."

"Only if you come on stage with me to be the scapegoat," Celeste says. I look down from the menu board as they stop right in front of me. Like we're a group.

Mickey scowls. He always seems to be on the verge of scowling. "I'm only going to see Cauler do his impressions and then I'm leaving."

"You're not staying for my cosplay? It's a surprise!"

"We are definitely not friends, remember?"

I don't have much experience with friends. But if there's one thing I remember about friendship, it's the constant back and forth, just like this. The comfort to poke at bruises without fear of leaving new marks.

I miss it. I haven't let myself miss it in years.

"You'll stay for my show, right?" I cut in like I've been a part of this entire conversation. "I know this is the first time we've ever spoken, but we are absolutely going to be friends."

Mickey looks skeptical, but before he can say anything, the barista calls out, "Corey!" I put on an oblivious smile at the accompanying sneer, and she watches me take my first sip like she's waiting for the coffee to burn through me like guilt. When I only smile and say "Thank you," she scoffs, shaking her head and getting back to work.

"Corey?" Celeste asks when I return to her side.

I add teeth to my smile. "Inside joke."

She looks at me blankly.

"Yeah, I know," I say with a laugh. "Another one who shouldn't do comedy at the talent show."

"And what are you going to do for it?" She looks me up and down like she's trying to suss out my hobbies based on how I dress.

I pass my coffee into my left hand and reach out to pull a coin from behind her ear with my right. She swats at her hair, and the coin is gone before my next sip.

"Maybe a little sleight of hand," I say. "Maybe some sword tricks. I don't get to show those off as much. Campus safety might get upset if I start carrying longswords to class."

Celeste quirks an eyebrow, the corner of her lip twitching into a restrained smile. "How very roguish of you."

Mickey blatantly ignores us in favor of texting until his name is called for coffee. He comes back with Celeste's too, and the three of us step out of the café together. Campus is more awake now, a few people cutting around us when we walk too slow for them. A group heads into the dining hall together. I hook my thumbs around my backpack straps and keep my head held high, a small, crooked smirk on my lips for everyone who glances my way. If they expect me to be embarrassed, I will never let them see it.

Celeste is the one on her phone now, sipping her coffee as we walk, snorting a laugh every few seconds.

"What's so amusing?" Mickey asks.

She gestures at me with her cup, not looking up from her phone. "Some of these memes are actually hilarious. You should write about this moment for your personal narrative, Nathaniel."

I let the smirk drop off my face in favor of scrunching my nose in consideration. "Mmm, nah. There's nothing life-changing happening here. Makes more sense to talk about the time I jumped a fence during a police chase."

They both look at me, some emotion crossing Mickey's face in the form of utter bafflement. It sends a rush of satisfaction through my blood. I feel myself genuinely smiling for once.

"Definitely a watershed kind of moment," I say. "Picking a lock on someone's front door in broad daylight and a cop car pulls up and they call out to me, *Forget your keys?* But like, in a way that I knew they knew, you know? So I took off running. Got a couple blocks, decided to cut back to throw them off, figured I was tall enough to clear this picket fence, but my foot got caught and I fell on my face, broke my wrist, and the cops got me."

I stop there. I could go on. Tell them about the trip to the hospital to get my wrist cast, how the cops and doctors together decided a weekend in the ward would do me better than a trip to jail once they got a look under my sleeves.

The whole story makes sense for the public speaking assignment. *Write and present a personal narrative describing a defining moment in your life. The moment you believe made you who you are today.*

But even summarizing it like that, omitting those key details, leaves an aching weight in my throat. Wipes that smile off my face like I've never before smiled in my life.

Celeste and Mickey are both looking at me expectantly, and I realize I kind of dropped off the face of the earth for a second there. I blink a few times, shake my head before forcing on a brand-new smile.

"Yeah, anyway," I say. "Definitely more speech-worthy than jumping out a window for the memes."

The two of them exchange a look like they're thinking *Haha, what the fuck?* Like they don't know if they should laugh or be concerned, or maybe back far, far away from me.

Celeste slips her phone into her back pocket, eyebrows pinned halfway up her forehead. "Well. Guess I'll have to look forward to your speech to hear the rest of it, huh? Maybe find something more interesting to talk about myself. See ya later, Nathaniel."

Mickey mumbles a *later* of his own, and they both branch off toward the science building. I have to make a conscious effort not to let my chin fall to my chest, my shoulders slump. I swallow against the emotion clogging up my esophagus.

Thinking about that day shouldn't make me feel like this. It took a couple years to get here, but that day set me up to become who I am today.

And I *like* who I am.

CHAPTER 3

THE SCRATCHES ON MY arm are shallow enough to heal quickly, but deep enough that they itch like hell as they do.

Maybe it's just in my head.

I close my hand around the worst of them and squeeze. Avoid scratching at all costs. My eyes stay fixed on Professor Greene as she gives her lecture, but fuck if I've taken in anything she's said in the past hour. My head is not in this classroom. I don't even think it's on this plane of existence.

A light jab at my bicep draws me back in like a lasso around the neck. I turn my head to look at the girl sitting to my left.

"Your leg is shaking the whole table," she whispers. "I'm trying to take notes."

I plant my heels on the floor. Cross my legs at the ankles under my chair. Put my elbows on the table and chin in my hands.

Dramaturgy. That's what Professor Greene is talking about. The sociological theory that basically claims the world is a stage and all human interaction is a performance. Simple enough to understand. Interesting enough that I *should* be able to focus.

But my arm is *so itchy*. It's a feeling I was once so used to it never phased me. But I promised myself college would be different. I'd remake myself and never bleed again.

This . . . this is dangerous.

"Are you okay?" the girl to my left asks. I can't tell if she's genuinely concerned or if she feels obligated to ask after calling out my obvious anxiety.

I smile at her, aiming for something casual and confident, but it doesn't feel right. Too big, too much teeth. "I'm good."

She looks me up and down, slowly and deliberately, eyes lingering on the death grip I have around my wrist. "Sure," she says before turning back to Professor Greene and her notes.

My own notebook is pushed to the very edge of the table in front of me, my pen barely within reach off to the right. I drag them both closer and poise pen over paper, ready to concentrate. Actively taking notes will keep my brain too busy to leave me.

I scribble the terms *self-presentation theory, impression management,* and *self-awareness vs. manipulation* and feel vaguely called out. Professor Greene and I make eye contact that feels too pointed, too meaningful. She can see right through me, right to the friendless, self-conscious kid I was through middle school, to the criminal I became in high school.

I bet she could analyze my every waking moment and make a neat little diagram of who I really am versus the self-presentation version I put out there for the world to see. She'd do it far more accurately than I ever could.

The end of the lecture can't come soon enough. I'm the first one out of my seat as Professor Greene dismisses us, but I restrain myself from rushing out and making myself look like more of a mess than I already do. That's not the *impression* I'm trying to give off here.

I tuck my hands into my armpits, pressing them tight against my body to hold them in place, stop them from wandering back to the scratches. It feels like everyone I pass is looking at me. I thrived on it this morning, but right now, I can't take it. I can't have them seeing through me like this. I keep my eyes on the sidewalk in front of me and hurry back to my room.

My roommate's not in, which isn't exactly surprising but *is* a little disappointing. I don't like him, we don't speak to each other even when he is in the room—I'm pretty sure he thinks I'm a disgrace—but his presence would at least be enough to keep me from doing something I'd only end up regretting.

I toss my backpack into my desk chair and sink onto the edge of my mattress, sitting on my hands and letting my shoulders relax as I exhale. There's creaking footsteps on the old wood floor outside the door, quiet conversation as a couple people pass by. I latch on to the sound, use it as an anchor until it fades and leaves me in empty silence.

It takes only seconds for the urge that's been simmering for days to boil over, surging to the forefront of my mind and staying there, loud and insistent.

I push myself to my feet so fast it makes me dizzy. Stand stock-still next to my bed, staring at the syllabi pinned to my roommate's wall, fists clenched tightly at my sides.

Maybe I should call my brother.

Or Mom.

Haven't talked to either of them in weeks. Seth is in the navy, training to be on a submarine one day or something like that, so I'm sure he's got some good stories. It's always funny listening to Mom tell Dad about all the wild shit she sees as an ER nurse.

Dad is out of the question. Mom's not great, with the way she tries to paint over everything she doesn't like about me like a stubborn smudge of dirt on her bright white walls. The way she talks about me to others reminds me of how she spritzes her houseplants with water and vinegar to make them look less dead.

Dad, though? I swear that man got a master's degree in hypocrisy, the way he rages about my criminal history as if he didn't spend half of his high school years in juvenile detention. Acting like I'm such a stain on the family name when he's the one who tainted it first.

His phone's rung three times before I even realize I've clicked through to call Seth. I hold it away from my ear, watching the screen, the word *ringing* blinking over his contact name for thirty more seconds before going to voicemail. Maybe he's in class. Some mandatory workout. Doing navy things.

Ignoring my existence, because we are family, after all.

It's not that Seth and I don't get along. Not exactly. We simply have little reason to communicate beyond blood. He's always been quiet and polite and well-behaved, while I ran circles around him, leaving chaos in my wake. Our parents tried so hard to put him on this pedestal, something for me to look up to, strive to be like, while I always kept my eyes anywhere but on him.

We have nothing in common anymore. Nothing to talk about.

I wince at a sudden sharp pain. Look down to find myself scratching at the scabs, one of them torn slightly open and beading with blood. My heart lurches out of my chest. I yank my sleeve back into place, down until it engulfs my fingertips, puts a barrier between my nails and my skin as I head out the door.

It's colder than I remember. In the time I spent in my room, a good half an inch of snow has built up, falling in heavy flakes that cling to me as I walk. The air bites at my knees, exposed through the tears in my jeans, and seeps through all three layers of shirts I'm wearing. But I don't go back for a coat. If I go back, I'll stay there and it won't end well.

I trudge down the hill toward the main road, leaving ruts in the snow behind me, and take a long walk off campus.

If I had a therapist, I'm sure they'd be very proud of me. Taking myself out of a dangerous, tempting situation.

If I had anyone other than myself, they'd be proud.

But all I have is me. And me? Well, I don't feel much of anything for him.

The world around me is muted. My head stuffed up like I'm wearing earplugs too deep. Cars pass too closely as I follow the curve of a guardrail with no sidewalk, and I don't notice until the cold splash of muddy slush hits the back of my legs.

It's like I'm staring down an extra-long hallway. The way perspective shifts and the end seems so, so far away and I feel so, so insignificant.

I lose myself there, barely conscious of the distance covered, the time passed, my own body. By the time I come out of it, the sun has reached the other side of the lake. I'm not walking anymore. I don't bother taking in my surroundings. It doesn't matter. All I know is there's a crumbling stone wall stabbing at me through my jeans where I sit cross-legged, arms draped over my knees, red from the cold. The lake stretches out just feet in front of me.

I feel heavy. Like a dozen weighted blankets have been piled on top of me. I let myself sink under the weight of it, here but not.

No one comes looking for me.

No one ever has.

CHAPTER 4

I FEEL LESS LIKE I'm deteriorating after a few days, as the scratches close up and the scabs dissolve, leaving behind faint pink lines amid fainter white scars.

I skipped class for two straight days and only left my room to use the bathroom, but I made it through, and that means something.

I need it to mean something.

I paint my nails with a fresh coat of black polish on Thursday morning. Dab eye shadow under my eyes to cover the natural dark circles with something I can call a choice. Separate my hair down the middle, picking out mismatched strands determined to stray to the wrong side, then scrub my hands through both sections to give it a careless, bird's nest kind of look. I slip into my layers, clip chains to my belt loops, and fill the many holes in my ears with dangling silver and black jewelry. Only then am I ready for people to see me again.

There's a moment as I pass by the café where I consider

going in to look for Celeste and Mickey, but I don't have a borrowed drink card this time and no money to get anything honestly. So I head right to class and sit at the table they've been sharing from the beginning of the semester, crossing my fingers the other guy who sits here doesn't come in first.

I plant my elbows on the table and clasp my hands in front of my mouth and watch the door as my classmates file in. I hear Celeste before I see her, saying, "You can't say something like that and not give details. That's just rude."

"I'm not convinced you're not selling everything I say to the NHL Network," Mickey argues.

That's when it clicks. The reason I'd heard his name around campus before I ever met him. He's not an influencer or thirst trapper—he's a hockey player. I've never been too big on hockey myself, even growing up outside of Buffalo. I don't like to watch sports in general. Not even lacrosse, and that was my whole world for a while there. If I'm not playing, I don't care.

Celeste and Mickey step into view, iced coffees in hand even as they're bundled up with snow in their hair. Mickey stops outside the door to let Celeste in first as she says, "Ooh, how much do you think I'd get?"

"Pennies," Mickey mutters, but Celeste has already spotted me, her attention immediately shifting. She smiles in the near-mocking way I'm already coming to expect from her.

"Look who's decided to come to class for once," she says,

pulling out the middle chair. Mickey slouches into his seat and guzzles down his coffee as he scrolls through his phone.

"I miss one day and suddenly my character is being called into question?" I say.

"Hm . . ." Celeste squints at me, rolling her lips together as she thinks. "Pretty sure you missed, like, the whole first week of class."

"That doesn't count. Syllabus week is optional."

"You sure you weren't just passed out in a bush somewhere that week?"

I squint at her in return before looking over her head at Mickey. "Is she this mean to everyone?"

He shrugs, not looking up from his phone. "My sister warned me she's mean to people she likes."

I quirk an eyebrow. "Ooh, in that case, hurt me more, please."

Celeste's smile breaks into something almost fiendish, while Mickey chokes on his coffee, spluttering it onto the front of his white hoodie.

Someone bumps the table and I look up to find the guy that usually sits here staring down at me. I smile innocently back up at him.

"That's been my seat all semester, dude," he says, tired aggravation in his voice.

"You can see the board better from my old seat." I gesture across the room to my abandoned table.

The guy's lip curls as he looks at me, eyes lingering on the earrings and the makeup, the nail polish. He glances sideways at Celeste before giving me one final scathing look and turning away to take my open seat.

I lean in closer to Celeste. "Mm, sorry. Didn't mean to break up your relationship."

She shakes her head and waves a hand in dismissal. "Honestly, I should thank you. I've been trying to get rid of him for weeks."

Professor Huang comes in then, arms full with a laptop and a stack of papers. She sets the laptop on the empty table she always claims at the front of the room and starts handing back our last assignment.

"Nicely done, everyone," she says, barely glancing at each person as she matches the paper to the student. "I'm very impressed with these outlines."

She stops in front of me and starts to hand over a paper, doing a double take before turning to scan the room for Celeste's man instead.

"Go ahead and read the comments I've left," she continues, "and we'll spend class today discussing how we can translate the outline to the performance."

She hands a few more papers back before returning to me and passing over my assignment, a seam down the middle and curled corners from the time it spent carelessly folded in my backpack. I peel back the top pages to find Professor Huang's comments at the bottom of the last.

The casual tone is very entertaining, but ultimately inappropriate for the informative speech. This would work well for the persuasive speech and your personal narrative, but this particular speech should sound more academic. You are a fantastic storyteller, Nathaniel. Perhaps consider taking a creative nonfiction course next year?

I tilt my head and read it again.

Huh. Creative nonfiction.

If I were to write stories about my life, where would I start?

Maybe with sweet, innocent toddler Nathaniel running around having sword fights with sticks, following his brother around like the squire to his knight. We made a tunnel through the underbrush in the woods behind our nonna's house, leading to a small clearing where we set up logs like thrones, dug a pit we made muddy stews in. It was a portal to our own little fantasy realm, until the older cousins found out about it and took over, banishing me but letting Seth in just fine.

Skip ahead a few years to preteen Nathaniel, acting out

and talking back and no one—*no one*—understanding why. Mom and Dad tried to be patient at first, but when none of their groundings or withheld privileges made a difference, it led to raised voices, arguments that bordered on violent but never fully crossed the line. A lot of shouted, *What is wrong with you*'s but never a calm, serious talk about it.

A nice segue into high school Nathaniel's crime spree, his fallout with his only friend, his epic breakdown, the end of everything.

Or maybe I'll start here. With me. Nathaniel Conti 2.0.

A tug on my hair dumps me back into my body, slouched halfway down in my chair and staring blankly out the window. Scraps of paper litter the table in front of me, the corners of my assignment folded and unfolded to the point of breaking off.

Celeste stands behind her chair, Mickey looking at me from over her shoulder. The rest of the room is empty.

"You planning on staying here all day?" Celeste asks.

I blink at her, slipping a hand into my pocket to feel the rounded corners of my deck of cards. Tug on the rubber band holding it together until my head feels less hazy.

I shrug. "It's cozy."

"Cozier in the library." She nudges my arm. "I'm meeting Tasha there now to get some work done. You strike me as the kind of person who needs to be reminded to do homework."

"*Oof.*" I hunch my shoulders like she's struck a blow right to my gut and look to Mickey. "She really likes me, huh?"

"Think she might be in love," he deadpans.

Celeste rolls her eyes, smiling slightly as she turns for the door, still talking like she knows we'll follow. "I simply do not want to see you drop out, Nathaniel. You're far too entertaining."

My blood buzzes through me. I would do just about anything to keep her entertained and interested.

Including skipping my afternoon class to hang out in the library with her and Tasha.

Mickey waves awkwardly as he continues on past the bridge to the library, and Celeste stops to frown after him for a second. I watch her watch him, then look over to see him with his shoulders hiked up and his head down as he marches away, then back to her.

"You sure it's not *him* you're in love with?" I say.

She screws up her face, a quick flash of disgust in the way she curls her lip before reining it back in and shaking her head. "It's not that. It's just . . ."

She trails off, and when I raise an eyebrow to prompt her to continue, she flaps her hand at me.

"Don't worry about it." Something about the tired tone of her voice stops me from pressing for more. She doesn't seem to shy away from gossip, so this must not be a gossiping matter.

She leads me across the bridge into the library, through an open space filled with study carrels and tables, dimly lit overhead with individual lamps at each study space. It feels like a dark academia movie set. I half expect to hear the distant sound of a crackling fireplace and gothic music drifting in from the ether, but there's only the turning of pages and pencils scratching against paper, the occasional sniffle or restrained cough.

We move into endless rows of bookshelves, and I remember why I don't like to come in here.

If I weren't following right at Celeste's heels, I'd lose myself. With books pressing in on both sides, no glimpse of a world outside, this space doesn't feel real. A minute could pass or an hour and they would both feel the same.

I keep my eyes on the back of Celeste's shoes and try not to suffocate, until she turns into a small gap in the shelves and up a short set of curved steps into a study loft. It *is* cozy. Closed off from the rest of the library by a brick half wall, low-set armchairs that look like they'll swallow a person up are set around a short hexagonal table.

Tasha's already here, chunky black boots up on the table, fishnets peeking through tears in their black jeans. They smile brightly when we come up the stairs, eyes locking on me as I trail in behind Celeste.

"Ah, Nathaniel! I didn't know you'd be joining us."

"I've been kidnapped," I say.

Celeste rolls her eyes, dropping her backpack on the floor at her feet as she sinks into one of the chairs. It does, in fact, swallow her up. "Yes, clearly, look at how much distress he's in."

I collapse into a chair with a huff. It's even lower than I anticipated, and my dramatic exhale becomes more of an undignified yelp when gravity takes hold. Celeste gives me a flat look as she rummages through her bag for her laptop.

Tasha keeps that smile on their face and offers me an open bag of Swedish Fish. I grin shyly back at them and cup both hands for them to pour the candy into, then lean back in the chair as I pop one into my mouth.

"So this is how you spend your weekday afternoons?" I make a show of taking it all in—the high, exposed beams of the library's ceiling far above us, the glass walls allowing shafts of sunlight to peek over the walls of the otherwise low light of the study cubby. Every breath smells like I have my face shoved into the yellowing pages of an ancient textbook. "Classes aren't enough?"

"This may come as a surprise to you, but we are, in fact, college students." Celeste doesn't look at me as she speaks, focused on the notebook she flips open and clicking a pen on her thigh. "And we take it seriously."

"We don't get much time for homework during the week," Tasha adds. They sit up straight, planting their boots on the floor and setting the bag of candy on the table. They pull their laptop closer. "Like tonight, we get on a bus at four thirty for a game that starts at seven and we won't be back to campus till around eleven."

Celeste slaps her notebook down on the table. "Homework on a bus ride? No thanks. I get motion sick."

It could be softball. It could be an ongoing winter sport. But I have a feeling.

"Lacrosse?" I ask.

Tasha smiles again. "Mm-hmm!"

"Huh. Funny. I used to play." It feels like an understatement. I didn't just *play* lacrosse. I lived for it.

Celeste leans forward, arms on her knees, curiosity overtaking homework. "Oh yeah? What position?"

"Attack. Pretty good too."

"Good enough to be a Royal?"

"I mean, seventh-grade varsity, set a league assist record sophomore year."

She cocks her head to the side. "Why aren't you still playing then?"

"Ah, well." I rub the back of my head, wincing. "Got kicked off the team junior year. Can't get recruited if you can't play."

A ray of sunlight cuts across the lower half of Celeste's face, leaving her narrowed eyes in shadow. It only adds to the judgment I feel her leveling at me.

"You really are a delinquent."

Tasha slaps her lightly on the thigh. "Celeste! Rude!"

"True, though," I say with a shrug. "Spent more time in handcuffs than lax gloves, kinda screwed my team out of a sectionals appearance, y'know."

I keep it nonchalant, voice carefree and body language relaxed, but my heart beats a little harder, squeezing like it's trying to wring out the anxiety before it can take root.

Talking about myself is one of my favorite pastimes. Just . . . not about my regrets.

We'd had a rough season up to that point, with our starting goalie moving away in November, long before lacrosse even started, but two more wins would've at least gotten us through to sectionals. I pretty much carried the team, setting up half the goals we scored. Without me, they didn't stand a chance.

Things could be so different now if I'd been able to talk my coach and principal down, convince them to keep me on the team. I didn't even *succeed* in breaking and entering, or get in any real trouble with the cops that time. If they could look past the whole court appearance back in the fall, they could've looked past this.

I had so much going for me, with lacrosse.

Less student loan debt in my future, with an athletic scholarship.

A reason to get out of bed in the morning, with 6 A.M. practices.

Maybe a bit of pride from my parents.

I catch myself just as a frown begins to take shape, shaking my head to divert the too-deep thoughts. I force a smile as Celeste and Tasha both look at me with evident curiosity.

"Well, give us the details." Celeste beckons with a twist of her wrist. "Something to do with that police chase?"

Tasha's eyebrows shoot up to hide behind their bangs. "Police chase?"

I reach for another candy fish and give them my slyest grin. "Google me."

Celeste *tsks*. "If you were a minor, that'll tell us nothing."

"What a shame."

She continues to give me that judging look, humming to herself, until I take out my cards and start going through every flourished shuffle and twirl I have mastered. It's a nervous habit. Something to keep my hands busy and my mind focused.

But no one needs to know that. Let them think I'm simply showing off. It fits the narrative better.

"In due time," Celeste says, watching the cards flutter through my hands, "all will be revealed."

CHAPTER 5

NONE OF US GETS any work done.

Celeste pretends, for a little while, keeping her eyes on her laptop and her notes while Tasha and I talk, but when I mention my family, her nosiness prevails.

"You have a brother?" she asks. Her laptop balances crookedly on her knees, one leg tucked under her and the other stretched out onto the table.

I waterfall the cards from one hand to the other. "Technically, yeah."

"Technically," she repeats.

"Yeah, I mean, we have the same parents and we shared a bedroom growing up, but we're not, like . . . brotherly."

I blank for a second.

I know Seth and I were close when we were very young. Back when we had the clearing in the woods and our sword fights. But that's all I really remember. Most of my childhood is lost to me, trapped behind some kind of mental block.

I can't remember how it felt to have Seth as more than an inconvenient roommate.

Honestly, when I think of brotherhood, it's not Seth that comes to mind.

It's turning out pockets and upending shopping bags to compare hauls after wandering through a mall on a Sunday afternoon. Someone to laugh with after getting jump scared by a creaking screen door while walking back from the gas station long after dark.

Quiet conversations on the shores of Lake Ontario, feeling loose and sleepy, safe enough to almost let a bit of honesty slip through.

It's a bond imbedded so deeply that when it breaks, every bit of sinew holding you together snaps with it, leaving you to unravel.

Brotherhood is pain and guilt and regret, and I absolutely do not want to think about that right now. So I finally shrug and say, "I don't know, aren't brothers supposed to watch out for each other? In an *only I can beat up my brother* kind of way? Seth and I mostly just ignore each other."

Celeste screws her face up at me, setting her laptop aside as she sits up. "Why?"

"Why what?"

"Celeste is studying to be a therapist," Tasha cuts in. They toss a fish at Celeste, and she lets it bounce off her shoulder without notice.

"Wow, that explains a lot, actually," I say.

"Yeah, she just has to work on her subtlety."

Celeste flaps her hand, brushing off the topic change as she leans forward with her forearms on her thighs, still locked in on me. "I don't understand siblings who aren't close. They're like built-in friends."

"Every family is different, Celeste," Tasha says. There's this cautious tone to their voice that I haven't heard from them before, and that paired with the intensity of Celeste's focus on me gets my mind going.

I open my mouth, take a breath to ask what I'm missing. Celeste doesn't shy away from asking personal questions, after all.

But I know the kind of trauma that can be dredged up by seemingly innocuous questions, and even if that's not what's going on here, I don't think I want to risk it.

I tuck my chin, fan out my cards in time with a slow inhale. "We're very different people," I say. "Seth's in the military, married, probably gonna have a kid in the next couple years. I'm just . . . well, me. We wouldn't be friends if we weren't family, so there's no point trying to force it just because we're related."

"That's fair," Tasha jumps in to say before Celeste can respond. They lean forward and turn their head to look at her so I can't see their face. Celeste watches whatever Tasha mouths to her, or maybe just reads their expression, and rolls her eyes.

"Not my problem anyway," she grumbles, then settles back into her homework.

Not her problem and not her business, I want to tell her. But that would be unnecessarily aggressive.

Tasha gives me a sympathetic look and a small shrug, and I brush the whole thing off with a shrug of my own.

Conversation effectively dies there.

Celeste and Tasha turn their focus to their homework, and I don't want to leave and make it seem like I'm bothered by whatever the hell just happened.

So I dig through my backpack, find my tattered copy of *The Presentation of Self in Everyday Life*, and flip through the pages, ready to be called out some more.

CHAPTER 6

nottasha
you free this afternoon?

natticon
always

nottasha
impromptu grunge photoshoot in the
leach basement?

natticon
absolutely

TRUE TO MY WORD, I gather up my grungiest clothing items
and accessories and head over to the Leach dorm after standing at my window staring at the lake for an hour, eating a bag
of Funyuns for lunch.

Tasha and Celeste are already in the basement lounge,
set up around the pool table. Celeste leans forward with her
elbows on the faded green fabric, scrolling through her phone
and lazily rolling a lollipop in her mouth while Tasha seems to
be begging her for something.

"Please, Celeste, *please* tell me you're joking."

Celeste pulls the lollipop from her mouth with a smack of her lips. "Nope," she says, popping the *p*.

"The point is to be sexy!"

"Slenderman can be sexy."

"*That*"—Tasha jabs their finger at Celeste's phone—"is not sexy. It's terrifying."

Celeste grins as she sets the lollipop back on her tongue, and I hop the last step toward them, slinging my backpack onto the pool table and standing across from them with my hands in my pockets.

"What about terrifyingly sexy?" I say.

They both look at me, Celeste once again removing the lollipop to point it at me and say, "Exactly."

Tasha shakes their head emphatically. "No. Absolutely not. The theme is *Things That Go Bump in the Night*. That implies, like . . . vampires. A standard, sexy monster."

"If they wanted everyone to show up as vampires, they would have themed it *Dracula's Brides* or something."

"What are we talking about?" I cut in again.

"Erotic Ball is in a few weeks and Tasha doesn't approve of my costume idea," Celeste explains, tone flat.

Ah, yes. Erotic Ball. One of Hartland's many themed dances, this time inherently horny. I wasn't planning on going myself.

"Oh, I'm totally going as a vampire," I say. "I'm halfway

there on a regular day anyway, and you can't get more sexy than that when it comes to the paranormal."

Tasha slaps Celeste lightly on the arm with the back of their hand. "See!"

Celeste drops her shoulder, lip curled. "Ugh, show some originality, both of you."

"You could totally make Slenderman hot, though," I add. "I mean, he has tentacles—practically does the work for you."

"Exactly," she says again, with finality this time, then crooks a finger at me and leads me over to the couches, sitting me down. She pulls the square coffee table closer and sits in front of me, the table legs creaking and shifting under her.

"Can I go through your bag to get outfits ready?" Tasha calls from the pool table.

"Yeah, but I take no responsibility for anything else you find in there."

Tasha laughs lightly, and I take a better look around the lounge, getting a sense of why they chose this location for a grunge shoot. It's in desperate need of an update, a decade or two behind some of the other communal spaces on campus. I toy with a fray in the dirty red couch cushion beneath me. The TV on the wall has a line of dead pixels running through the middle. There's a collection of empty liquor bottles and beer cans on the TV stand below it and the garbage in the corner is overflowing, a folded pizza box balancing precariously on top of the tower of trash. The block windows at the top of the wall barely let in sunlight, leaving the lounge in a dusky fluorescent haze from the tube lamps hanging from the ceiling.

It's a different vibe from the library, but it has the same effect, making me feel more and more liminal with every detail. Like I'm sinking into unreality.

If all human interaction is a performance, these are the backstage spaces. The spaces where the act deteriorates so completely, you don't know who you're supposed to be, if you even exist anymore.

I don't know how long Celeste is waving her hand in front of my face before I jolt back into myself. She pulls her hand away, shooting a look at Tasha, who settled onto the couch beside me at some point, their legs folded under them.

"Sorry," I say. My voice is far more strained than I'd like it to be. "Zoned for a second there."

The quirk of Celeste's eyebrow implies it was a lot more than a second. She has a makeup kit on the table beside her. A whole chest, open with tiers, that I never noticed her bring out.

Neither of them comment. Celeste raises both hands, framing my face without touching. With Valentine's Day behind us, she's changed her nails to a deep green with lighter vines painted along the edges.

"Can I?" she asks.

I glance at the makeup kit, then at her serious, tight-lipped expression. Her snark is typically matched with a perfect blankness on her face, but this feels different.

Is she asking if she can do my makeup, or is she asking if she can touch me?

Why would she ask to touch me?

"Yes?" I say to both.

She keeps looking at me for a long, drawn-out moment, like she's trying to suss out my deepest, most personal thoughts. I raise an eyebrow and, finally, she rests her fingers on either side of my jaw, tilting my head in every direction as she studies my face.

I huff a laugh. "Am I a suitable canvas?"

"Perfect," Tasha says. I glance sideways at them, a smirk tugging up the corner of my mouth. Their head must catch up with their mouth then, because their eyes widen and a blush rises on their cheeks. "Perfect for what we need."

"You have a big-ass nose," Celeste deadpans before I can respond.

"I'm Italian," I say.

She scoffs, but when she brushes her thumbs under my eyes, it's the most gentle and overtly caring touch I've ever felt. "You need to sleep more, Conti."

My mind blanks. For a second I think I might be dying, with the way my heart folds in on itself, sending sparks of shock through my bloodstream. My hand prods at my chest like I'm expecting it to collapse—I'm so goddamn unaccustomed to being cared for.

My voice is raw when I speak. "Last name basis, are we, Hernandez?"

"Nathaniel is too much. I could do Nate, if you'd prefer."

I open my mouth to suggest my real nickname, but my chest does another pulse of that heart attack feeling. No one's used that name for me in years. It would never sound right on anyone else's voice.

"Please, no," I say.

Celeste hums thoughtfully and gets to work dusting powders onto my face, accentuating my sunken cheeks and tired eyes, then drawing black liner around them in a much more involved design than the simple lines I usually do myself.

With a pointy object aimed directly at my eyeball, she says, "Uh, hey, sorry for making things weird in the library."

"Oh, you noticed, huh?"

She frowns slightly, then descends with the eyeliner pencil once more, forcing me to close my eyes. "It's just that family things are kinda . . . well, touchy for me."

I want to ask her to elaborate, being as nosey as she is, but she's being so nice and I just want it to last. So I go with, "Same, honestly," and leave it at that.

"Right. Glad that's behind us." She caps the eyeliner and sets it aside with everything else she's used on my face, into a tray to be cleaned, and uncaps a jar of greenish hair gel.

She scoops it into her hands and runs her fingers through my hair until it falls just the way she wants it.

"How'd the game go last night, anyway?" I ask.

"We won," she says, curling a lock of my hair around her finger. "Obviously."

She doesn't offer up any more details, and I have to remind myself to breathe when she leans in close, lips pursed in concentration, fingertips on the bottom of my jaw to hold my head in place.

I once put makeup on someone like this. He didn't know how to do it himself, but he wanted to know if he could pull it off. If it would suit him as well as it suits me.

He sat on the lid of the toilet in the only bathroom in my house, and I held his face the way Celeste holds mine, his eyes closed and his lips parted, completely at ease, trusting me far more than I deserved.

It did suit him. Maybe even more than it does me.

A month later, I saw him for the last time, bruises around the eyes instead of liner. I wonder if he still does it sometimes. If he's learned to put it on himself or if he found someone else to do it for him.

Someone healthier for him.

"Hey, this sexy vampire costume," I say in a rush of breath, desperate for a different train of thought. "I want to be covered in teeth marks."

Celeste grins wickedly, a flash of teeth, until Tasha says,

"I'm sure Celeste can do that for you." Her fingers drop away from my jaw and we both turn our heads to gape at them.

They look up from the shirt they're folding in their lap, blinking when they see the way we're staring. "What?"

"I am a lesbian, Tasha," Celeste says. "I'm not putting my teeth anywhere near him."

Tasha blushes all the way to the tips of their ears. "Oh my god, I meant with makeup!"

I cock my head to the side. "But where's the authenticity?"

Tasha drops their chin to give me an incredulous look. "You want someone to bite you hard enough to leave marks?"

I shrug one shoulder. "I'd let you do it."

Their blush turns furious, and Celeste rolls her eyes so hard they go full white.

"Get a room," she says. "Nasty."

The words came out easily enough, but now that they're hanging there in the space between us, I feel kind of . . . dirty. I've never so much as kissed anyone before. Sex sounds fun in theory. *Looks* fun on the screen of my phone. But the thought of anyone touching me other than myself makes my stomach want to turn inside out.

"Oh my—" Tasha cuts themself off as they slap their hand over their face, but they're fighting a smile. "Are you done, Celeste?"

She sighs like she's trying to sound annoyed, even though she's clearly amused if her faint smile means anything, and gives my face a final inspection. She twists her wrist at me. "That's about as good as I can do, given the subject."

I smile at her with all my teeth and Tasha flings the first outfit at me to get us moving.

I get changed in the laundry room by the stairs. It's a lot of black and chains and layers, chokers and earrings, pretty much exactly what I would wear on an average day with a little extra Tasha flair. They fuss over me some more, adjusting my clothes and my hair before setting me up on the couch again. They talk me through the poses they want at first, adjusting every little detail, but once I get the idea of what they want—loose and lazy and arrogant—I start moving on my own after every few shutter clicks.

After the couch, they lay me out on top of the pool table, standing over me with their feet on either side of my hips to get top-down shots, a king of hearts between my fingers, the rest of the deck scattered around me.

Each photo seems to broaden Tasha's smile, earn more genuine praise, and I feel myself come alive. The longer it goes on, the less the cockiness they want from me is an act.

It's the same rush I feel when I pocket something that doesn't belong to me and walk away unscathed. When people gawk at my card flourishes and sword twirls. It only gets better when Celeste starts throwing in her own begrudging compliments. Two pairs of eyes on me, marveling at an ability I didn't even know I possessed.

But I know it's not all on me. Standing behind Tasha and looking over their shoulder as they click through what they've taken so far, it's obvious that they have an eye for composition. I know nothing about photography, but I know that if they were to put the camera in someone else's hands, me in identical poses, the end product wouldn't be the same.

"This your major?" I ask.

Tasha shakes their head. A warm vanilla scent wafts from their hair. "Minor. My parents are making me study education. As if teachers actually make enough to live off of."

"Would you even want to be a teacher?"

Their scroll through the photos slows, and they're quiet for a moment. When they do speak, their voice is small.

"I don't know. Sometimes I think I might. It's more stable, even if it doesn't pay, and I mean, half the girls my older sister graduated with call themselves photographers now. But this is what I've always wanted to do. I want to tell stories with these photos."

Celeste appears at my side, pressing a stack of clothes to my chest. "Do this next."

I step back into the laundry room and strip off all the top layers before actually taking a look at the outfit Celeste's put together. This one is simpler. A dingy-looking cream-colored sweater vest and black-and-white checkered pants with chains.

But.

It's just the vest.

I hate how instantly and violently the joy and excitement rips from me. The protective way my right hand curls around my left wrist.

I don't care if they see. I don't care what they think. What anyone thinks.

I don't.

Close my eyes. Breathe in slow and deep. Steady myself so my voice doesn't shake when I peek out from the laundry room and say, "This looks better with layers. Something with sleeves."

"It's not about what looks better," Celeste says from her place sitting on the back of one of the couches. She doesn't glance away from the TV. "We're creating a character."

"Just saying, my arms aren't very nice to look at. Very pale and noodley."

She finally looks over her shoulder at me, blank and serious again. "Isn't that the aesthetic you're going for?"

I don't answer fast enough. They expect quick wit and when I don't deliver it, they share a wary look between them.

Don't let them jump to conclusions.

"But I don't wanna step on your creative vision. I can make it work, it's fine." The words bleed together with how quickly they spill out of me. I dig my nails into the doorframe and swallow the anxiety building at the back of my throat.

It's fine. They won't see anything. And even if they do, it doesn't matter. The scars are old. I've recovered. Nothing to worry about.

Before either of them argue—if they even would—I duck back into the room and pull the vest on over my head, careful not to mess up Celeste's work on my hair. When it's situated, I move to change into the next pair of pants, only to see Celeste's arm sticking into the room, holding out a denim jacket. The rest of her is hidden around the wall. Giving me privacy.

I chew the inside of my cheek. Squeeze my hand around my wrist. They're going to think I'm so messed up. That I have things to hide.

I gingerly take the jacket.

Mutter a *Thank you.*

"No worries," she says, and then she's gone.

She was right about the outfit. It's a better character design without the jacket. But I *feel* the difference as soon as my arms are covered. The nerves evaporate like they never existed, and I walk back out like I didn't nearly have a breakdown.

Celeste is trying to start my hair on fire with her eyes, she's looking at me so intensely as I approach. I refuse to falter, keeping my wince fully internal. Tasha gives me a sideways glance and smiles as they flash the screen of their camera at me.

"You should thank your ancestors for your bone structure," they say. "It's very good on camera."

I grin at them. Run a finger along my jaw. "I'm sure you could make anyone seem photogenic, but yes, my bone structure is exquisite."

They worry at their bottom lip, eyes roving over my face before seeming to come to a decision. The wrinkle between their eyebrows smooths out, and their eyes flash with some emotion I can't place. They nod sagely. "Could slice bread with that jawline."

Celeste gags. "Get. A. Room."

Tasha's grin is as sharp as I've ever seen it. I mirror it back to them.

And everything is good.

CHAPTER 7

SATURDAY NIGHT, INSTEAD OF crashing a party, inserting myself into strangers' conversations, and being a general nuisance, I sort through my sword collection. There's replicas from video games and movies and shows. Full-sized longswords that make for epic spins and flourishes. Smallswords for when I want to get fancy with some dual-wielding.

My roommate eyeballs me from his desk chair as I lay them out on the floor between our beds. I'd already stowed them away in my closet before he showed up on move-in day in August, so this is the first time he's seeing them, and he does not seem impressed. He watches me for a few minutes before slowly—quietly—standing and leaving the room.

He'll probably report me to campus safety, but these swords are only dense foam and plastic. The real ones are back home, locked up in my parents' room the way they have been since junior year, even though they're not sharp enough to do any major damage.

I don't know why they bothered taking them from me at all. Did they really think I would've used them on myself?

Would they honestly have even cared?

I frown so deeply I feel it in my entire face. Of course they would care. They may not love me, may not even like me at all, but I'm still their son. They would feel my absence. I know they want to see me do better, not cease to exist entirely.

Logically, I know that. But I don't doubt for a second that they've considered how much simpler their lives would be without me.

But my parents are two hours away and I don't need to be thinking about them right now. I have a college campus to impress.

I sit back on my heels, tapping my fingers against my knees as I look over the spread before me, trying to decide which to bring to the talent show. The obvious answer is the lightsaber. It'll put on the best show, get a better reaction. But it cost me almost every cent I earned working at the golf course and if I'm rusty and break it on stage in front of everyone, I might actually die.

Maybe it'll be like riding a bike?

Fuck it. I'll give it a few swings out in the hall and everything will come back to me.

I stuff the foam swords back in the closet and drag the lightsaber case out from under my bed. Put on the most Sith-like clothes I own, a billowy black cloak I bought for sword fights in the woods and tight black everything else, and go a little overboard with eyeliner and dark eye shadow all around my eyes. I feel a little like Anakin giving in to the Dark Side as I walk through the halls of my dorm, testing the weight of my saber with the bitchiest look I can muster on my face.

It takes a second to realize someone's calling my name as I descend the stairs, the cloak trailing on the steps behind me. I blink a couple times, snapping myself out of character before turning to look up the stairs. Tasha's coming down, a camera bag hanging from their shoulder.

They're dressed in a baggy off-white button-down tucked into black cargo pants, a silver chain hanging from their belt loops, a slouchy burgundy beanie. They look just as good as ever, and when they smile at me from their vantage point half a staircase above me, there's an unfamiliar twist in my gut.

"Wow, you look great!" they say, taking in my over-the-top outfit with wide, dark eyes.

"Not as great as you." The words burst out of me before I can think better of them, and I turn away in case the heat I feel rising in my cheeks is visible under all the makeup.

Tasha falls into step beside me with a cheerful, "Thank you! I know it throws some people off when they see me like this, since I usually present pretty femme. Sometimes I just want to look like an emo teenage boy, you know?"

I nod once. "Understandable. It's a good look."

Their nose crinkles with their smile. "You *would* think so."

My phone vibrates in my pocket and I have to push aside the cloak and several draped layers of black to get to it.

Seth's name in my phone is just *Brother*. I wonder what he has me in his contacts under. Probably my full name. A formal *Nathaniel Conti*.

He sent a picture of a rapier, with a fancy basket hilt, and the message: *One of my shipmates just got this. thought you'd like it.*

His messages are always pictures. A blurry US Navy cap held up by his socked foot, accompanied by the message: *Sometimes it feels like cosplay.* A picture of his lunch tray with: *Almost as good as high school's taco asserole.*

Sometimes I ignore them, no idea what I'm supposed to say in response. Sometimes I'll send back a picture of whatever I happen to be looking at in the moment. The bare branches of a tree outside my dorm window. My feet dangling over the lake.

We don't know how to just ... talk to each other anymore. We haven't for a long time.

Now, I stop just inside the door leading out to the cold and snap a picture of the lightsaber held out in front of me, unlit, and send it to him without comment.

"You showing off a talent tonight?" I ask Tasha as I put my phone away.

They shake their head and I step outside first, holding the door for them. "Nah, my talents don't make for good stage material." They tug on the strap of their camera bag. "I *will* be putting them in the art show later this semester, though."

The student union is just across the path from this back exit to our building, so we duck our heads against the lashing winter wind and jog over. Tasha holds the door for me this time as I bundle the cloak around me. We stand together in the entryway, kicking snow off our shoes. The ambient hum of dozens of people speaking all at once bleeds through the doors closing off the main room from the cold of the small foyer.

I feel anxiety trying to take hold, sparking in my chest and pulsing out with each heartbeat. I take a shallow breath and shake out my hair.

Don't let the sparks catch.

"Do you mostly do things like . . ." I motion toward myself, waving my hand around as I search for the right word. "What we did the other day? Portraits?"

Tasha's chuckle is strained, like they're self-conscious about it. "Ah. I'm still pretty new at this, so I'm trying to find my niche. But the thing Celeste said about building a character? Those are the shoots I really love to do. Especially, like, fantasy shoots. Making people look like they're adventurers in a tabletop RPG, you know?"

"Oh, hell yeah, that's awesome. I've never played before, but I love the concept."

Their smile broadens with excitement, like they're not used to a positive reaction. "Maybe you can be in one of the shoots sometime?" They lift a hand toward my head, pausing until I duck slightly to give them permission and an easier reach. They fix my windblown hair, moving strands to their proper side as they talk. "That's how me and Celeste became such good friends outside of lacrosse, actually. She does fantasy cosplay and I take the pictures for her. We're trying to get a group together for a campaign too. Just need to find someone willing to run it."

I look up at them through my lashes as they continue to pluck at my hair. Their smile brings out the roundness of their face, the plump of their cheeks. This warm feeling blooms in my chest. Something I haven't felt in a long time, and only for one other person.

Something like affection.

They're standing here in the cold vestibule with me, fixing my hair and sharing their joy and I don't think I want it to end.

When I came back to campus this semester, I made the decision to be seen by this entire student body. It didn't matter how they saw me as long as they did.

But Tasha and Celeste . . . they make me want to be more than seen. They make me want to be *known*.

"I would love to be in one of your fantasy shoots," I say,

more earnestly than they have ever heard me. "I can even supply the swords."

They finish with my hair, positively beaming at me as I straighten back up.

"Excellent," they say. The hum of voices rises into a cheer, a single booming voice over a crackling loudspeaker welcoming the first brave freshman to the stage. Tasha glances over their shoulder before offering me a hand. "C'mon! We'll miss it!"

I decide, here and now, as my fingers lace through Tasha's, that no matter what mold I force myself into from here on out, this version of myself will be friends with them.

It's been too long since I had a friend.

SOME GUY DOES a cardistry show, and I'm at once relieved I went with the lightsaber for the sake of originality and disappointed that I won't have the chance to show him up.

I'm much better than him. Probably had more free time to practice, more incentive to keep my hands busy.

A girl plays a hurdy-gurdy while dancing barefoot across the stage.

Another shows off how long she can hold a handstand,

which is way too long if you ask me. By the time she drops back to her feet, I'm the one left feeling like all the blood has rushed to my head.

The guy Mickey must've been talking about . . . Cauler, he said, right? He comes out to raucous cheers from the other side of the room, dressed in all black, asking the crowd to name celebrities and campus figures and impersonating them flawlessly.

I'm up after a couple does a dramatic reading of some viral internet blowup, acting out the conversation with their whole being.

They dim the lights for me at my request, and I stand in the shadows with the hood of my cloak pulled low over my face, waiting for the music to build before I step out.

Is this too much?

They'll like the lightsaber tricks just fine, I'm sure. Even if they're not into Star Wars, it's fun and flashy, especially with the lights down. But maybe I shouldn't have gone so far as the outfit, the dramatics. Maybe that's too cringe. Too try-hard.

Too much. Am I too much?

I almost miss my cue, having to force myself into *I don't give a fuck* mode to get my feet moving in time. I step slowly out of the shadows, face hidden in the oversized hood, putting out the most menacing vibes I can conjure.

The saber lights gradually at the press of a button, hilt to tip, Sith red, and when I start twirling it around my hand, spinning it behind my back, tossing it in the air and swinging it like I'm dancing more than fighting, the crowd eats it up.

I know I'm good at this. I know I make it look easy. I have hours' worth of videos hidden away in my TikTok drafts of me doing sword tricks to trending sounds that I never found the nerve to hit *post* on. I've watched them myself a hundred times, enough to scrutinize every movement, enough to know that, *yes*, this is a talent of mine.

It's a useless talent, sure, but I'll take it.

I leave the stage vibrating with adrenaline, half-ready to find Tasha in the crowd and sweep them off their feet to draw out the rush. Mass post all those videos stuck in my drafts. Become a real-life Sith Lord.

A hand brushes my arm as I descend the steps off the stage and I flinch as it pulls me down from my attention high. Yennefer of Vengerberg, the Witcher 3 version, is standing in front of me. It takes a couple of blinks for me to see Celeste behind the costume, it's so fucking good, her black and white traveling clothes an almost exact replica. A shiny black wig cascades to her shoulders in thick waves.

Her eyes—violet contacts and all—narrow at my startled reaction, and she eases her hand off my arm. I catch a whiff of flowery, fruity perfume. She's cosplaying all the way down to the scent.

"If I knew you were going Star Wars," she says, "I would've brought out my Second Sister cosplay."

"Damn. Maybe we can stage a battle on the dock, let Tasha get some good pictures."

Celeste purses her lips to the side and looks away, off to the guy doing stand-up comedy onstage. "I'm not good with lightsabers and swords. I can make costumes and pose for pictures, but that's it."

I scoff. "That's it? This is . . . ," I trail off, gesturing to her whole being.

"Impressive? Perfect? Stunning? Yes, I know."

I press my mouth into a thin smirk, humming noncommittally. She rolls her eyes and crosses her arms, leaning back into a perfect Yennefer stance.

"Awesome," I say. "Incredible." I take a step away, turn before she can react, and return to Tasha at the back of the room to watch Celeste's show. Tasha clings to my arm, giving me an excitable shake, their grip tightening as they bounce on their toes when Celeste takes the stage to lip-sync and act along with a Yennefer scene.

Because, yeah, all she can do is make costumes and pose for pictures.

I look down at Tasha, the affection and joy in their eyes

as they watch Celeste. Then back to Celeste, showing off her immense talent.

I only met them a week ago. I barely know either of them. They sure as hell don't know me.

I don't even know myself.

But they make me feel solid for the first time in years.

CHAPTER 8

I'M IN TASHA'S ROOM later, watching them edit some of their photos.

They didn't invite me, exactly. It just kind of happened. Celeste lives in a different building than us, and we walked back to ours alone together. A lot of people are having parties tonight, or going down to Ithaca, which I would normally be all over. But Tasha has morning practice, and we weren't done talking when we got to my floor, so I stuck with them to their door and they left it open for me, mid-sentence.

I think they're expecting something to happen.

I think they *want* it to.

We're on their bed, sitting with our backs against the wall, their laptop open in their lap, and we've gotten closer and closer until now they're leaning against me, their shoulder pressed to my bicep, their knee on my thigh.

They're talking, explaining the steps as they work, but I am not processing any of it. I think I'm responding the way they want, if their smiles and laughter mean anything, but my head and my body are at such a disconnect, I have very little idea of what I'm saying.

There's a framed photo of their high school lacrosse team on their desk, all crowded around a massive trophy, eye black painted on their faces and mud on their knees. A small non-binary pride flag sticks out of the soil of a potted plant beside it. Most of the wall behind us is plastered in wrinkled and torn handmade posters in different styles, made by different people, for Shen Girls' Lacrosse #13, Tasha, with a little witch hat drawn beside their name on each one. Art and photos are arranged through it all, actual high-quality prints, not the computer paper everything on my wall is printed on. Above the head of the bed is one poster-sized photo of an older Korean girl backlit by the sunrise, bunching the hem of her gauzy purple dress up by her thigh as she extends her leg, toes pointed, dipping them into the lake before her. What's left of the sunlight glints off the tall, pointed halo crown on her head.

"Nathaniel?" Tasha bumps their shoulder against me and I blink my way back into my body. They're looking at me closely, frowning. "You okay? Feel like I lost you for a second there."

I shake my head, jabbing my thumb over my shoulder. "I was wondering about . . . well, that."

They twist to look, using their hand on my thigh as leverage. It takes all my power to stay relaxed, to keep myself from tensing at the close contact, keep my breathing even.

"That?" they ask, brow furrowing in confusion for a

second before understanding dawns on them. "Ah, the *girls' lacrosse* thing. Yeah, those were made before I realized I'm not a girl. They have good memories attached to them, though, so I like to have them."

"Does it . . ." I swipe my sweating palms on my thighs, accidentally rubbing their hand. They move it out of the way. "Does it bother you? The women's lacrosse label now?"

They adjust so they're leaning their shoulder against the wall now, facing me, their knees wedged against my leg. "It depends. *Most* of the way I feel about gender depends, really. I'm fine being called part of the women's lax team when I'm with the girls, and I'm mostly fine with girls *seeing* me as one of them. But I hate being seen as a woman by men. And I want all nonbinary people to recognize me as one of them."

They give a little shrug and a sheepish, maybe even nervous, smile, like they're worried about how I'll respond. I take a moment to really absorb what they said, turn it over in my head. I don't want to be flippant about it.

"I think I understand," I say. "There's, like, safety levels involved, yeah?"

They nod. "That's part of it. Like, I could never be with a straight guy because I'd know the whole time he's thinking of me as a girl, you know?"

The question means something else. I can tell by the way their eyes flick down to my mouth. The slight lean in.

I swallow against the lump in my throat. I had a feeling

things were heading this way. I even helped lead us in this direction, subconsciously or not.

I lick my lips. "I don't think I'm straight," I say.

The corner of their mouth twitches into a smile as if to say *I don't think so either.*

And then they're leaning in.

White noise rings in my ears. My breath gets lost somewhere on its way down, as my stomach forces its way up into the space where my lungs should be.

They stop just an inch from contact, waiting for me to follow through or back off, a wordless question.

I raise a hand that trembles only slightly. Push my fingers into the hair at the nape of their neck. And I meet them halfway.

I've never done this before, but I try not to make it obvious. I take it slow, steady, rest my other hand gently on their collarbone, mouth closed until I feel their tongue against my lips and open up to them.

It feels nice. Not life-changing, earth-shattering, the way it's built up in the movies, by everyone in high school. But nice.

At least until my head catches up with what's happening and panic prickles across my skin.

Between one breath and the next, Tasha is in my lap, my head tilted back to stay with them. I let my hands fall to the curve of their waist, and they take my bottom lip between their teeth.

I like this. I do. I want this to happen. And I like Tasha enough that it should be okay. They're nice. They're attractive. They won't hurt me.

I want to do this.

But my stomach is a maelstrom. My throat is closing. An acidic burn sizzles at the back of my tongue.

Tasha pulls back, the absence of their mouth so sudden I forget to breathe for a second.

"Nathaniel?"

They sound concerned. I realize my eyes are squeezed shut, my hands fisted into the comforter. I have to forcibly relax my body, make a conscious effort to exhale and open my eyes.

Tasha's hair sticks out on the left side where my hand had been, their cheeks flushed. They're frowning again, eyebrows pinched.

"What's wrong?"

I try to laugh it off, but it comes out so obviously strained, there's no denying that I am far from okay.

They're out of my lap, sitting on the edge of the bed a heartbeat later, giving me space. I swallow, but the sick feeling lingers. It might even be getting worse. There's a cold sweat coming over me. My mouth waters.

When I finally find words, my voice is ragged. "I don't feel so good."

They stand fully from the mattress, wringing their hands together. "Water?"

"I—I think I should go."

"Okay, yeah, you—"

I'm off the bed, shoes in hand, in the hallway before I can hear the rest. In the bathroom dry-heaving over a toilet before I can make sure all the stalls are empty.

I've always been so good at shoving everything down. The memories. Not even shoving them down really, just . . . detaching myself from them. Like those things didn't happen to me at all.

Right now, they're fighting for a foothold. Like a hand holding my chin in place and forcing me to look while I desperately struggle to turn my head away from them.

The reason kissing someone I want to kiss could make me sick. The reason I turned into a shithead, a criminal, desperate for my parents to ask *why*. The reason why, in the long run, I lost my only friend.

I wonder if Gianna feels like this too. If her life is in shambles the way mine is.

I hope not. God, I hope not.

I sit back against the stall door, knees pulled up, heels of my hands pressed hard against my eyes.

Why is it that when I want to be gone, I can't? I don't want to be here, I don't want to feel this, but I can't seem to find that tether holding me inside my mind. The same one that has no problem fraying on its own.

I'm stuck. I'm stuck I'm—

My phone vibrates and I jam a hand into my pocket, stretching my leg straight and lifting my hip so I can get it out, nearly dropping it with the way my hands tremble as I unlock the screen.

nottasha
I'm so sorry Nathaniel
I shouldn't have taken it that far

I fully rely on autocorrect to get out a legible response.

natticon
no worries. Nothing to do with you
really just didn't feel good
sorry

I lean my head back against the door, stare up at the point where the wall meets the ceiling. And breathe.

I'm all right.

Absolutely fine.

THE THING IS, I really *don't* think I'm straight.

I don't know what I am.

I've been attracted to girls, I've been attracted to boys, I'm attracted to Tasha.

77

And I know that someday, I do want to be with someone that way, even if it really freaks me the fuck out at this point. Obviously.

So I don't think I'm ace.

It's just . . . trauma.

Trauma that I will continue to bury. I'll keep pretending, and one day, maybe it won't be pretend anymore. One day, after years and years of acting like I'm okay, I will be.

It starts with picking myself up off this bathroom floor. Splashing cold water on my face until it soaks the front of my shirt and leaves my hair dripping.

I brace myself on the sink and let the water run in rivulets down my jaw, staining the ceramic black from all the Sith makeup.

I'm okay.

Repeat it to myself until it's real.

I'm okay.

CHAPTER 9

I'M STILL OKAY WHEN I spend the rest of the weekend in my room, sitting on the edge of my bed shuffling a deck of cards to the point of tearing, and even when my Mom calls to ask how the first month of the semester is going and I say *Good, great, goodbye.*

I'm okay in class on Tuesday, listening to Celeste and Mickey banter back and forth.

I'm especially okay when I bump into Tasha in the stairwell, when they give me a pleading look and I smile, make a joke, avoid direct eye contact.

I'm okay when Celeste demands my presence at the lacrosse home opener Thursday night.

I'm maybe slightly less okay when I show up to the field, see the teams warming up, and get smacked in the face with nostalgia.

I really miss this fucking sport.

I spot Celeste instantly as she cuts through the 8-meter, catching a pass and whipping it into the net in one smooth motion. Her dark hair is piled on top of her head and held off her face with a purple-and-black headband.

I find Tasha a moment later, their hair tied back into two tiny pigtails, defending against an attacker behind the net.

It's hard to look at Tasha too long. Makes me feel this weird combination of shame and guilt and . . . I don't know. I don't know what it is exactly, but I don't think I like it.

Maybe I'm not a good person and maybe I don't deserve anything with Tasha anyway, but I know I don't deserve to feel like this.

I stand at the bottom of the bleachers with my arms draped over the fence until warm-ups are coming to an end and the teams start gathering at their benches below me. Someone steps up next to me, rattling the chain links.

Mickey James. He stands there quietly for a second, jaw tense like he's thinking incredibly hard. When he finally opens his mouth, his words fall out like they were gathered at the back of his teeth.

"Need somewhere to sit?"

I look over my shoulder at the crowded bleachers behind us. "Hmm, I don't know. I'm sure *someone* would make room for me."

Mickey gives me a flat look, a lazy blink. No wonder he and Celeste get along so well. He pushes away from the fence and heads back up the bleachers. I follow a step behind him, till we're close to the top, where three people watch our ascent like it's the whole reason for this gathering, never mind the big game.

One of them is the guy who did the impressions at the talent show. Cauler. He's Black, undeniably attractive with that intense jawline, his all-black style. His hands are jammed into the pockets of a black puffer jacket, stretched earlobes hang from his beanie, and his face glints with several piercings. He has his dark eyes locked on me as I stop behind Mickey.

"Shut up," Mickey says to the group as he drops onto the bench next to Cauler. None of them have said a word.

A white girl with pastel purple hair sits on the other side of Cauler, leaning forward to watch as I settle in beside Mickey. She shares a blanket over her lap with the Black girl next to her, who has both gloved hands wrapped around a steaming thermos. She sips, then gives me a small wave. I smile back and jerk my chin up in greeting.

Purple Hair Girl returns her attention to Mickey, giving him this fiendish kind of smirk. "Making friends all on your own, are you?"

Mickey sighs. Rolls his eyes. Mutters, "Kill me."

"The infamous e-boy," Cauler says. His eyes lose some of that intensity, and a corner of his mouth ticks up into a small, crooked smile.

I laugh. "Infamous, huh?"

"You did jump out a window. Nathaniel, right?"

"That's me."

"Jaysen." He glances at Mickey, sees the way he's sitting with his arms crossed and his shoulders hunched and his face all scowly, and nudges him with an elbow.

"I'm Delilah, since my brother doesn't care to introduce us," says the girl with the purple hair.

"Jade," says the other with another little wave. She passes the thermos to Delilah and flips open the sketchpad in her lap to a blank page. With the way she narrows her eyes at me, I'm pretty sure I just became the subject of an art project.

"You here to support your best friend Celeste?" I ask Mickey. Higher up in the bleachers, the wind is sharper, colder. I shove my hands in the pockets of my fleece-lined flannel and pull it tight around me.

Mickey's lip twitches like he wants to scowl some more, but he holds it in. "No. My sister." I glance over at Delilah. "My *other* sister."

"There are five of us," Delilah says with a shrug.

"Damn," I say. "Your parents were busy."

Mickey's lip curls, but the others grin, Delilah with a little snort of laughter. A voice comes over the speakers, broadcasting from the booth at the top of the bleachers, welcoming the crowd to the Royals Women's Lacrosse home opener, and starts announcing the starters for both teams, one of them being Bailey James.

The rest of the team lines up along the sideline to form a tunnel with their sticks for the starters to run through, Tasha and Celeste standing across from each other.

And then I'm thinking about Tasha again, and I really should not be doing that. I squeeze my hand around the deck of cards ever present in my pocket. Let the edges nip at my skin.

"I used to play lacrosse, y'know," I blurt out as the Royals win the opening draw and move down the field with a long pass.

Mickey perks up, turning his head slightly toward me without looking away from the game. "Yeah?"

"Traitor," Jaysen says under his breath. Something close to a smile flickers across Mickey's mouth.

"You don't look like a lax bro," Delilah says. I watch her eyes jump from my black-and-white hair escaping in tangles from my folded beanie to the silver dangling from my earlobes, to the chains on my pants clinking against the metal bleachers with every shift of my weight.

I smirk at her. "Oh, trust me, I leaned into the stereotype in the beginning. Not my finest hour."

I turn my attention back to the field as the whistle blows on a foul in the 8-meter and the Royals set up for a free position shot. The crowd erupts as the ball hits the back of the net a moment later, the goal scorer dropping her stick for the refs before being swallowed up by her teammates.

"Why don't you play anymore?" Mickey asks once the celebration ends and the game is back in motion.

A gust of freezing wind tenses my shoulders, forces me to squint and turn my face away from him until it passes. I've played lacrosse games in the middle of snowstorms. In twenty-degree weather. Absolutely miserable conditions where I stood there thinking *I will never be this cold again in my entire life.*

I never thought I would miss that.

But sitting here getting blasted by winter wind off the lake, with a lacrosse game playing out in front of me, I do.

I miss the game. I miss the camaraderie of a team. I miss the awe after a nasty play. I miss the potential my future held, with the eyes of college scouts on me.

"I got kicked off my team," I say. And usually . . . usually I'm able to sound so flippant about it. Like it didn't ruin me. Like it's just some quirky little anecdote about my life with no lingering impact.

Now, the bitterness seeps into my voice. Regret curls in my chest.

The four of them look at me expectantly, and as many

times as I've told the story without hesitation, even playing it up to add to the drama, I can't bring myself to do it now.

My cards will scatter in the wind if I try to bring them out now, but I need something to occupy my hands, focus my mind on anything but this. I find a quarter in the pocket of my flannel and dance it across my knuckles.

The conversation moves on when they realize I'm not going to elaborate. I don't think I've ever been grateful for someone *not* asking me about myself before now.

Jaysen leans in front of Mickey to watch the coin. Demonstrating it to him until the February air freezes the feeling out of my hands is enough to snap me out of broody mode, fade me back into the infamous e-boy persona they expect from me. Cocky, slightly unhinged, no fucks given.

And they eat it right up. Jaysen and Delilah laugh at every outrageous thing out of my mouth. Jade looks up from her sketchbook to give me smiles that scrunch her nose and eyes. Mickey face-palms.

I barely feel the cold.

The game ends with a Royals win, a goal from Celeste, and a few forced turnovers from Tasha. Most of the crowd stays put for the men's game to follow, either too loyal to leave or frozen to their seats, but I really don't need to stay here and watch the version of this sport that *I* played. Imagine myself in place of one of their attackers and spiral again.

I leave my audience of four behind to lean over the fence at the bottom of the bleachers, calling out to Celeste and Tasha at the team bench. Celeste looks over her shoulder as she pulls sweatpants over her leggings and game shorts, face flushed with exertion. She smiles faintly up at me, while Tasha quickly looks away, hiding in the hood of their team jacket.

It stings. It shouldn't sting. I feel just as awkward talking to them.

But I push through it, determined to be unaffected. "Throne Room for victory celebration?"

Celeste shakes her head. "We're obligated to stay for the men's game. You should too. We can get food after."

The men's team descends on the home bench as the women's team begins to clear out, dropping off jackets and bags and water bottles before taking to the field for their warm-up. For a second, I almost agree. I'm not so fragile that I can't handle sitting in the stands and talking to my friends while a lacrosse game plays out in front of me. That's ridiculous. I don't even have to watch.

But one of the goalies from the Royals men's team stops just behind Celeste and Tasha, towering over them with his unnecessary height, looking up at me.

With the helmet on his head, I can almost convince myself I'm seeing things.

There's no way.

No way.

He tugs off one of his gloves, hooks his fingers under his helmet, pulls it off, and there's no denying it.

Max Palazzola.

My ex–best friend. My *literal* ex–partner in crime. The guy who taught me what true brotherhood feels like.

I stand rooted to the spot. Eyes wide. Unbreathing.

I didn't know he was here. How did I not know he was here? Blocked on social media or not, how did I not hear his name on campus, catch a glimpse of him before now? Hartland isn't big enough to hide someone this important.

He looks almost the same as the last time I saw him, only less lanky now, like he's finally grown into those long-ass limbs. His light brown hair is shorter. It was almost to his shoulders before, a good flow out the back of his helmet. Now it's clean-cut, masculine, the way his dad always wanted.

And there are no bruises around his eyes.

He stares up at me with his mouth slightly open, looking just as shocked as I feel. My vision is so tunneled in on him that Celeste and Tasha could've evaporated and I wouldn't know it.

"Nat," Max says, and that single word brings the faded sound of our surroundings surging back in around me and cranks my heartbeat into overdrive.

I can't talk to Max.

I'm not even *allowed* to talk to Max.

I push away from the fence, turn so fast I almost slip on the cold metal bleachers.

Celeste calls after me as I go, but I can't stay here. Not at this game, not with Max right in front of me.

Maybe not at Hartland at all.

CHAPTER 10

I CALL MY MOM as soon as I'm back in my room, giving myself no time to talk myself out of it. She answers on the second ring.

"Nathaniel?" There's a worried pitch to her voice. "Is something wrong?"

I push my fingers through my hair, catching on wind-blown knots. "Why is that the first thing you think? Can't I just call you to talk?"

I hear the disapproving cluck of her tongue, and she changes her tone back to the typical impatience she has with me. "Nathaniel."

Because I never call just to talk.

I take a deep breath and let the words out on the exhale. "I'm dropping out."

"Like hell you are!" Dad barks down the phone. Of course she had me on speaker.

"I am," I say. "I'm not cut out for this—you know I'm not."

It's not entirely true. I've always had decent grades. Wasn't earning any academic honors, but I know how to pass a test and write a paper and breeze through school. I wouldn't have gotten into Hartland without lacrosse otherwise. But I can't be here anymore. Not with Max.

"So what are you gonna do, work at the golf course the rest of your life?"

A quick flash of anger burns through me at Dad's absolute hypocrisy. I can't help but match his aggressive tone. "You should be proud of me for taking after you."

"I want better for you!"

I wince, pulling the phone away from my ear at his shouting, but he's not done.

"You can do better, Nathaniel. If you'd put as much effort into *anything* as you do getting into trouble, or your pointless card tricks, you could do so much."

"Like what, Dad? What do you see me doing?" I sit on the edge of my bed. Stand and kick at a pile of dirty clothes on the floor. "Should I be a cop? Put all my criminal experience to use? Go play sailor with Seth?"

"And why not? We raised you the exact same—how the fuck did you come out like this?"

I sink into my creaky desk chair and put my head down on the desk. One day. One day they'll ask me something like that, ask me what's wrong with me, what the hell happened to make me like this, and I'll tell them. They won't believe me, they'll assume I'm full of shit, and I'll be justified in cutting them off and never looking back.

The background noise from the phone fades as Mom takes me off speaker, silencing Dad's raging. She sighs heavily. "I always thought you'd study something to do with sports. Go into coaching maybe, or, what is it, management? Sports management? Lacrosse has started, right? Why don't you see if you can volunteer with them?"

I stand so quickly the chair falls out from under me. "Absolutely not. I'm telling you, I'm dropping out. You can come pick me up this weekend, just get my stuff home and I'll figure it out from there. I'll put in overtime at the golf course and have a shitty apartment by the end of summer and you'll never have to see me again."

"You think that's what we want, Nathaniel?"

I think that's exactly what they want, but my throat feels too tight to get any more words out. I pick up the chair and set it gingerly back on its legs.

"Get through the semester and we'll talk about next year, all right?" Mom says.

I grumble my acquiescence and goodbyes, and toss my phone onto my bed.

I spent all of last semester in my room, ignorant to the fact that I shared a campus with Max. I don't want to hide away again. At least if I dropped out, really did spend all hours at the golf course, got an apartment, I could figure out a way to keep this act up. I could find myself in the nightlife or something.

I won't last till May doing the same thing I did in the fall. If I stay here, I'll lose myself for good.

IT'S BEEN MONTHS SINCE I last looked up Max online. I try my best to not even think about him most of the time.

But he's hard to forget.

Especially with the way our lives revolved around each other so completely from the moment we met to the moment it all fell apart.

I doubt he thinks of me. And if he does, I know it's not fondly.

I pace circles into the creaky hardwood, chewing a hangnail on my thumb. My roommate comes back as I'm in the middle of a lap around the space between our beds. He gives me a look like I'm absolutely insane, as if he's never experienced even a hint of anxiety in his life, grabs a change of clothes from his dresser, and heads back out.

I throw myself face down on my bed.

Did Max know I was here?

He couldn't have. He was just as stunned to see me as I

was to see him. If he'd known, he would've gone to another school. I *know* he must've been recruited by other teams. He's a phenomenal goalie. Probably had his pick of the list.

How did we both get here?

I pick my face up out of the pillow and swipe my phone unlocked, typing Max's name into every social media I remember him having before I can talk myself out of it. His old accounts are still there. And I'm still blocked on every single one of them.

Except Instagram.

He once had hundreds of followers. That account is gone, but there's a new one with his name and a profile picture of a lacrosse stick propped up against a helmet and gloves, just a handful of followers and a couple posts.

But I'm not blocked.

My thumb hovers over the screen, a bead of blood gathering in the crook of the nail from my chewing. There won't be much to see, sure. But it's *something*. I'm not blocked, that has to mean . . .

Nothing. It means nothing. He just hasn't thought of me to remember the need to block me on a new account.

I lock my phone again. Hold it against my chest. Spiral for a minute or two or twenty.

He has me blocked everywhere else. That's a clear sign that I'm not welcome to look into his life. This new profile was an oversight. I can't go snooping where I don't belong.

I do still have pictures of him on my account. I should respect him enough to get rid of them. Erase our history once and for all.

It's not hard to find the last post I made with him. I'm not as active on here as I'd like to be. My camera's never been good enough to produce the quality of content I'd want to.

The first picture I delete is one of me and Max in a haze of smoke, staring blank-faced down at the camera I'd propped against a wall and set on a ten-second timer. A half-burnt cigarette dangles from my fingers.

I don't hesitate. Not with that one or the next two: Max trying to tug his shoe out of his German shepherd's mouth. Max hanging upside down from a set of monkey bars.

I don't hesitate until I get to the first video. Max doing trick shots. Flipping a lacrosse stick over his head, catching it behind his back with the ball still in the pocket, all while smiling brightly and telling some outrageous story about owning a chicken farm in a past life. My laughter is loud and uncontrolled and genuine from behind the camera, and Max beams at me, smiling in that unique way of his. More in the eyes than the mouth.

I can't delete it. It's a snapshot of a moment of true happiness. No faking it. No persona. Just me and my best friend—my only friend—laughing together and not getting arrested while doing it.

I can't delete it.

I close out the app and set my phone down beside me.

Mr. Palazzola always blamed me. For corrupting Max. Like I wrote his criminal record for him.

Maybe I did.

I dragged him into my unhealthy coping mechanisms, my illegal attention grabs, because obviously the only way to get my parents to notice something was wrong was through shoplifting and pickpocketing and vandalism.

Max's dad told him to stop talking to me. More than once. Just like my parents threatened to ship me off to some home for troubled youth.

But they weren't asking the question that I needed them to ask, so I didn't let up. And because Max and I were so irrevocably entwined, he didn't either.

Not until a gun got involved. Not until we sat for hours together, handcuffed on a curb outside a convenience store with construction paper pumpkins and skeletons decorating the windows. Not until we stared juvie in the face and Max went home and came back to school with a black eye and never spoke a word to me again.

He was gone a few weeks later. Moved out of state or something. Never saw or heard from him again.

Until tonight.

I think I might've been hit by a bus.

I should call my brother. My real brother. He would know

how to handle this. He always knows exactly what to do in any given situation.

But I don't need a reminder of how stupid I am. How bad I am with people. How much of a failure I am always going to be.

So I hold off on that.

Instead, I roll onto my back. Stare at the ceiling. And I drift.

CHAPTER 11

TASHA KNOCKS ON MY door the next day.

I know I must look rough, judging by the way they wince at the sight of me. I rake my fingers through the knots in my hair and fake a yawn like I just rolled out of bed and haven't been sitting awake all night staring at the wall and forgetting to exist.

"Hey," I say through the yawn.

"Hey." They worry at their bottom lip, tug at the hem of their oversized sweater. "We didn't go to the Throne Room yesterday. Wanna go now?"

"Oh. You and me?"

They smile, but it's one of those forced smiles where the corners of their mouth pull straight back. "Celeste too."

I nod, a little too quickly. "Okay, yeah sure. I'll meet you there."

They blink. "Oh—okay. See you there, I guess."

I close the door, and only after the latch clicks do I realize they wanted me to walk with them. Hand still on the doorknob, I close my eyes and take a deep breath. This will be forever awkward if we don't talk about it.

They're halfway down the hall by the time I find the nerve to open the door and peek my head out, call their name. They turn to look at me, arms crossed over their chest like they're holding themself together.

"You wanna talk?" It's almost painful, forcing the words past my teeth. And if that's already this hard, the actual conversation is going to be torture. I've only just met them and they're already seeing past the persona I want *no one* to bypass.

Tasha bites their lip, eyebrows pinched as they look at me. They nod hesitantly and step in my direction. I back up into my room, leaving the door open for them and take a moment to straighten out the blankets on my bed, fold a stick of gum into my mouth. Try to seem even slightly put together.

They stand just inside the door after closing it behind them, holding onto their elbows and looking extremely uncomfortable.

Just . . . get it over with.

"S–sorry," I choke out.

They pull their head back, startled, blinking in confusion. "You have nothing to be sorry about, Nathaniel."

"I do, though. I know that"—I wave my hand vaguely between us—"whole thing probably made you feel like shit about yourself. You would've told Celeste otherwise, and she hasn't made a single snide comment about it, so I'm guessing you didn't."

Tasha slowly shakes their head. "I didn't. But . . . not because of that. She wouldn't make fun of you for this, and neither will I. It's not something to be ashamed of, not being ready. I'm the only one with something to be ashamed of here. I took it too far, too fast, and just assumed we were at the same pace. I'm sorry."

"What do you mean, not ready?" I say, too sharply, too defensively. "It's not like I've never . . ."

They give me this very small, sympathetic smile that kills the lie on my tongue. "You try very hard to act like a bad person," they say. "But I can tell you're not."

It's almost insulting. Like they're telling me that the person I want to be will never be enough to cover up who I really am. I'm not trying to act like a bad person. I'm trying to act like someone who doesn't care whether or not they are.

No.

I'm trying to *be* that someone.

And they're standing here saying I'm not. It makes me want to prove them wrong.

I tuck my chin, look at them through my eyelashes, and lower my voice. "We're at the same pace, Tasha. And I feel better. I'm up for it right now, if you are."

They sigh softly, their smile knowing. "Celeste is waiting."

They back out into the hall while I get dressed. I spend too much time staring at the makeup and jewelry piled on top of my dresser, debating if I should do my usual or forgo it entirely, walk out barefaced.

Maybe there's a compromise here. I don't have to fully hide myself away in my room again. I can simply keep a lower profile so Max doesn't have to hear about some outrageous thing that Nathaniel guy did over the weekend. Don't stand out, don't be obnoxiously noticeable, but don't isolate.

Or I could go ahead and drop out. I'm eighteen—I don't need my parents' permission. If Mr. Palazzola finds out I'm here, he'll pull Max anyway, and he belongs here far more than I do.

Tasha smiles again when I finally come out into the hall, nothing flashy about me but a single pair of earrings and my hair. Their smile seems at least half-genuine this time, but they don't speak as we head for the stairs.

I'll have to be the unaffected one. "How are the pictures coming along?" I ask.

They perk up, gaining an inch when they straighten their spine and pull their shoulders back. "Great! You really are a natural."

"Think your followers will like me?" I give them a playful nudge with my elbow, and they laugh softly, a faint blush rising on their full cheeks.

"They're going to eat you up. Might have to make you a regular."

"You'll have to start paying me then."

They give me a wan smile. "We'll see what happens."

We pull our hoods up and brace for the cold before stepping outside, once again jogging across the path to the student union. Celeste is already inside, sitting in a booth in the Throne Room, typing on her phone. She looks up as we approach, then stands to meet us, stopping directly in front of me.

She crosses her arms and leans in, looking me up and down. Studying me like an insect pinned to a board.

I lean in with her, close enough to be almost nose-to-nose. "What?"

"Are you and Max exes?"

I pull back, blinking. "What makes you think that?"

"The way he talked about you last night."

I feel all color drain from my face, leaving me light-headed.

"Maybe we should get our food first," Tasha cuts in. "We can talk about this while we eat."

I would rather not talk about it at all, but I know that's not an option. Not when it comes to Celeste and her need to know everything.

We order plates of loaded fries and pizza logs and

mozzarella sticks and the two of them sit across from me in the booth like I'm about to be interrogated.

But I have a question for them first.

"How did he talk about me?"

Celeste purses her lips, drumming her fingers on the table. Tasha dunks a mozzarella stick into marinara sauce, over and over.

"He asked if we've been hanging out with you," they say softly. "If you're doing okay."

I break a pizza log in half. Squeeze until grease leaks over my fingers.

"It's not even *what* he said," Celeste elaborates. "It's how he said it. The look on his face."

I shake my head. I don't need to know. I don't need to be thinking about that. It'll only complicate things. "Well, we're not exes the way you're thinking. He was my best friend."

"What happened?"

I take a bite and chew slowly. The crispy fried pizza taste takes me back to early high school, when Max and I would walk to the sub shop down the road from school before practice, order shit that would make us throw up if Coach pushed us too hard.

"How much has he told you about himself?" I ask. I don't want to give away anything he's not comfortable sharing.

"We don't know him very well," Tasha says. "He mostly kept to himself and his team last semester."

"We do know he has a criminal record," Celeste adds with a pointed look, one eyebrow raised. "He's pretty open about that, how far he's come, whatever. But he never mentioned . . ." She trails off, that eyebrow slowly lowering as she realizes what she's about to say might hurt me.

And it does. I feel it like a needle pushed slowly into the center of my chest.

Of course Max wouldn't mention me. It shouldn't hurt. He's moved on and that's a good thing.

"Me," I finish for her. Celeste nods, focusing intently on the plate of fries between us. "Yeah. I don't blame him. I didn't even warn him the first time I actually stole from a store. That was . . . seventh grade, I think? Didn't warn him then and just assumed he'd keep playing along every other time. He always tried to take all the blame."

And I always let him.

"You know about the jail incident?" I ask.

They both nod. "He never went into detail," Tasha mutters.

I tear another chunk off my pizza log, and the filling spills out onto the napkin on the table. "Halloween, junior year. That was the last straw. We were charged with armed robbery and his dad forbid him from ever speaking to me again. Moved him away a month later."

Not that he would've wanted to speak to me ever again anyway.

Celeste's eyes bulge. "Armed robbery? How'd you get out of that one?"

I shrug listlessly. "Good lawyer? Being teenage white boys? I never actually took the knife out. Just something I always carried on me, so when they found it in their pat down, it turned into this big deal."

That knife staying in my pocket didn't only save us from juvie. Pretty sure if I'd taken it out, the gun the store owner held in my face would've become much more than a threat.

"But you should know," I continue, "Max is a good person. I was always the instigator."

I slowly reach for another pizza log, only to tear it apart like the first. Keep my face as neutral as possible because if I try for my usual smirkiness, it'll be so painfully obvious that I am a fraud.

"We couldn't talk to him much yesterday because of the game," Tasha says quietly, not looking at me directly. "But . . . now that the season's started, we're going to be spending a lot of time with the men's team. If we invite you to parties . . ."

I nod once, my head too heavy to pick up for another. "Yeah. That's good. You should get to know him. I mean, he's great. You can . . . you can choose him, it's fine. You *should* choose him. I'm just . . ."

"That's not what they meant," Celeste says. She sounds vaguely annoyed with my self-pity, with me.

The sudden pressure behind my eyes gets me on my feet quicker than if someone had started shouting *Fire*.

"Nathaniel." Tasha reaches for my sleeve, stopping before touching me, curling their fingers. "You—"

"Thanks for the food." I keep my chin tucked to my chest as I leave them behind.

Neither of them calls out to me.

CHAPTER 12

MONDAY MORNING, I DRESS in black sweatpants and a nondescript black hoodie under my winter flannel. Hide my hair as best I can under a generic baseball cap. Forgo the makeup and the earrings and the chains. Become your average, everyday male college freshman. Do not stand out.

It goes against everything I've wanted for myself this semester, but I need to do it for Max.

The way he looked at me the day he came back to school after our arrest . . . that shit still haunts me. The bruises around his eyes were almost faded, but the spark of life in them was just. Gone. I tried so hard to make sure he was okay, but he wouldn't acknowledge me, kept walking when I tried to stop him in the hall, clenched his jaw and pushed past me when I stood right in front of him.

He didn't look at me again. Not even once. And then a few weeks later, he was gone.

Now *I* need to be gone. I never want to see him like that again, even if it means never seeing him at all.

But now that I know he's here, I see him *everywhere*. Stepping into the café as I head to class. Across the dining hall during lunch. As I turn the corner into the hall where my sociology class is, standing outside the door talking to Professor Greene.

I turn on my heel. Skip class and hide out in my room the rest of the day. Keep my head down the next time I go out.

People aren't looking at me with interest anymore. I become old news, another face in the crowd. That's the whole point, but I can *feel* the drain on my willingness to even exist without the eyes on me.

It's too much, right? I don't care what people think of me, so why do I rely so heavily on them thinking about me at all? Why don't I feel real when I'm alone? When no one's looking at me. Why do I need external validation, or else fade out of existence entirely?

And well . . . I miss the almost friends I've made and lost. It was only a couple of weeks, but I'd gotten used to walking to class with Celeste, meeting Tasha at lunch, passing notes with Celeste during our classmates' speeches. Even flirting with Tasha, despite that brutal hiccup we had.

Without them, I fall back into the self-isolation of last semester. No compromise, just a total shutdown.

I have nothing to do with my time except for homework and card tricks. I hole myself up in my room with days' worth of dry cereal I snuck out of the dining hall and make my way methodically through each syllabus, using the internet to guide me through things I haven't learned yet. Barely worrying about quality and grades, just using it to pass the hours.

After each assignment, I take a break to practice a new card flourish, then get right back to it.

It's the personal narrative that drives all that momentum to a grinding halt. Every time I set down my cards and try to focus on writing about the police chase that cost me lacrosse, my brain only wants to linger on the arrest that took Max away from me.

It was my idea, just like all the others, and it wasn't well thought out. Not in the slightest. It was never supposed to be as serious as it became. Just for fun, to see if we could pull it off. Do it to say we did it kind of thing, and hey, if we did get caught, maybe it would be just big enough to open my parents' eyes.

Never big enough to implode everything.

Max, tall and clumsy as he was, knocks over a display case of breakable novelty cups, draws the cashier over to help clean up. While he's distracted, I reach across the counter and open the register. Wasn't expecting the owner of the place to be in the back doing inventory.

The only reason I know what happened next is because they showed the CCTV footage in court. As soon as the gun was in my face, I was gone. My body stood there, hands held out in front of me, but even the grainy security feed could see how completely absent I was behind the eyes.

That's probably why the knife stayed in my pocket.

I hate that I don't remember the last moments I could call Max my friend. I hate it more that he does. That his last memory of us together is something so fucked.

I'm sitting at my desk, desperately trying to shift my thought process anywhere else, when everything starts to blur out around me. I try to fight it. Keep working, keep typing, stay here, but I feel so foggy I have to stop and press my fingers against my eyes. Take a second to try to find my footing again.

I reach for the deck of cards on the desk beside my laptop, but when the fog clears enough to see through, I'm in the middle of my room with my roommate standing in front of me, waving a hand in my face.

I flinch back a step and he mirrors the movement, raising an arm to shield his face like I might hit him. When no violence comes, he scoffs. "Are you high?"

"Yes," I say. Because the alternative is the truth and the truth is that I am not well.

And those are words I will never speak aloud.

He throws his hands up in exasperation. "Can you not do that in our room? I'm not gonna be the one responsible for keeping an eye on you and I'm definitely not taking the fall when you get caught."

"Sorry."

He scoffs again, then puckers his mouth like he tasted something sour. I wait for him to turn away, and then I go back to my laptop.

The screen is still awake, the cursor blinking halfway down an empty page like I sat there with my finger on the *enter* button, watching the pages scroll. I snap the lid shut and go to bed.

I stay there for a whole day, only leaving when I absolutely have to use the bathroom. Even then, part of me feels like it stays behind, buried in the blankets.

Dissociation is weird, okay? There are times when it drags me so far down, I worry I'll lose half my lifetime to it. Moments where I *need* to be here, to get work done, to feel things. Times where I think I'm doing pretty okay and I still fracture. It scares me the most then.

And then there are times where I welcome it, even wish for it. Like in that bathroom stall after the thing with Tasha.

Because whenever I come fully out of it, those rare moments where I'm fully conscious in my own being, I realize I don't like myself very much. And when you stay with that feeling too long, well, it tends to blot out everything else.

By the time I force myself to face the Hartland student body again on Friday, February has given way to March, and I'm absolutely sick with hunger. I almost pass out in the shower. I stop by the dining hall for a single slice of buttered toast, taking small nibbles as I walk to class. It's all I can stomach.

I had to get up and go to class today or risk losing letter grades, but my head still feels like it's floating about five inches off my shoulders and I'm not present enough to pay attention to my surroundings. Max is only ten feet in front of me when I finally notice him, looking me right in the eye.

My heart leaps halfway up my throat, feet skidding to a stop on the icy sidewalk, a complete freeze in fight or flight for a good three seconds before I whip my head around in search of a place to hide.

"Don't even think about it, Nat."

I stop breathing. Pull my arms in close to my body, fists clenched so tightly around my backpack straps that my fingers ache. Hike my shoulders up to my ears and duck my head and make myself as small and nonthreatening as possible in front of him.

He stops just out of reach, the crowd of students parting around us as they pass. I have never wanted to disappear the way I do now.

We stand silent for several long, tense moments. I feel his eyes on my face even as I keep mine fixed firmly to the ground at his feet. His sneakers are so white. Not even the muddy slush across campus has touched them.

"You've been avoiding me," he finally says.

I let out a breath through my teeth, blink several times

just to be sure he's not going to dissipate into mist right in front of my eyes. My heart is beating too fast, too shallow, and I get that same nauseous, light-headed feeling I had this morning, in the steam of the shower on an empty stomach.

"Well . . ." My voice is so small. "Yeah."

I hate that this is what he's reduced me to. I want to be able to laugh about this, even if it's forced. I want to put on that cocky grin I've perfected and be untouched.

Maybe I could, if this had been his fault. If I didn't have guilt devouring me from the inside out.

Max sighs. "You done with classes for the day?"

I nod, even though it's a lie. Even though my day is just starting.

"Walk with me."

It's not a question, or a suggestion. He steps around me, guiding me back in the direction I came from, and I follow as instantly as he's always followed me. I stay several steps behind, dragging my feet just to feel the connection to the ground beneath me.

Max takes us to the dining hall, into the small room separated from the main hall by a massive fireplace. It's quieter here, with most people gathering at the long tables on the other side. Private enough for an uncomfortable conversation, public enough that it soothes some of the vulnerability.

He takes a seat at the corner table, under large, frosted windows looking out over the lake. I ease myself into a chair across from him, take out my cards like a survival instinct, tapping the bottom of the deck against the table.

The minutes drag on, no sound between us but the drone of voices and laughter from the main hall, the clang of pots and pans and shouting from the kitchen.

I steal a glance at Max. I thought I'd never see him again. Put him so far out of my mind I refused to even acknowledge his presence in my memories. I made him into a nameless, amorphous thing, shadowing me through the school day, hovering beside me in the back seat of the bus to away games, sitting on a closed toilet in my bathroom as I dabbed makeup where his face would be. A presence over my shoulder as I pocketed things at the mall, got caught with spray paint in hand.

But it was always Max, and trying to erase him like that wasn't fair to him. He deserves to be remembered, no matter how much it hurts.

He takes a sharp breath, and I brace myself.

"Coach kick you from the team for that?" he asks.

No need to elaborate. *That* could only mean one thing.

I split the deck in two. Shuffle the cards against the table. My voice catches when I try to respond. I clear my throat, take a moment to collect myself before speaking.

"No," I say. "Not until I got myself into trouble during the season."

"Junior year still? Surprised you're here if you weren't

recruited. You were always so anti-college unless lacrosse was involved."

"Mom and Dad were convinced it was this or prison, so . . ." I shrug. They were probably right.

"Still, would've expected you to do community college. At least a state school. Why put yourself into all that debt for something you don't even want?"

I laugh humorlessly. "You know my parents, Max. They're nothing if not elitist hypocrites. Is this really what you want to talk about right now?"

He shakes his head, shifting in his chair to pull a leg up under him, giving him more height over me. He knocks his knuckles on the table, motioning for me to deal the cards.

I set up our go-to legal pastime. Rummy. We fall into it so casually, like we're sitting in our high school library during sixth period study hall with nothing better to do.

"How have you been?" he asks.

I lift my chin to look at him fully. Instinct tells me to lie, to put on a show, that things have been great, that *I've* been great. I've given too much of myself away already, by hiding from him, shrinking at his approach. I can still recover from this, get it together and put on the face I want the world to see.

I try. Stretch my lips across my teeth and smile, smile, smile. Even squint a little to make it look more real, like it reaches my eyes.

"I'm great," I say. "College suits me better than I ever expected."

Max gives me a flat look, eyes never leaving my face as he discards, ending his turn. "Just as full of shit as ever, I see."

The smile drops off my face, settling into something that screams, *Don't open, dead inside.*

"That's more like it," Max says.

I draw a card and match his lifeless tone. "What ever happened to 'fake it till you make it'?" I lay down a run of *two, three, four* and discard a ten.

"I don't think that works for what you've got going on up here." He reaches up as if to poke me on the forehead, but I shy away from the touch. He curls his finger back into his fist before dropping it to the table.

I look back down at my hand, wait for him to finish his turn before drawing a card and melding a trio of jacks, adding a five to my run. If this were a couple years ago, we'd both cheat our way through this game and I would win because I've always been better at sleight of hand.

But Celeste and Tasha said he's been telling people he's come a long way from his high school crime spree, and maybe that doesn't extend toward friendly card games, but I don't want to be the one to test it.

"I really am good," I try again. "Just laying low these past few days."

"Avoiding me," Max corrects me.

"Yes." Frustration bleeds into my voice, draws my eyebrows in together. "You have me blocked on everything—I figured that meant I should stay away."

It's not an accusation, but he winces like it is, turns his face toward the windows as he takes a slow breath in. "I haven't used any of those accounts since I moved. I've thought about messaging you, but . . ." He shrugs. "Couldn't seem to find the nerve. Seeing you here kinda felt like a kick in the ass, like why didn't I reach out to you as soon as I could?"

I give a rough shake of my head. "You should've pretended you never saw me. I'm not trying to get you in trouble with your dad."

I grimace at myself. I don't need to remind him of his dad's temper. He's probably doing his best not to think about it, being away from him for the first time in his life.

But Max huffs a laugh. "My dad is in Albany. His drone is too cheap to make it this far to spy on me." He lays down several cards, but I'm too busy looking at his face to count what's left in his hand. He's got this wry grin going, but I stare blankly back at him. "I'm kidding, Nat. Relax. He hasn't hit me again. Not since we left."

"Because I wasn't around to provoke him. I haven't changed, Max. You shouldn't be talking to me."

"So what are your plans for tonight then?" he asks, quirking an eyebrow when I only continue to stare. "You haven't changed, right? So you're gonna be stealing from the bookstore, maybe breaking into dorm rooms or admin offices, trashing the faculty commons? Need a lookout?"

I cut a hand through the air between us. "No! No. I don't do that shit anymore. Not since I got kicked off the team."

"I'd call that a change, then."

I heave an irritated sigh and open my mouth to argue, but he levels a hard look at me, as serious as I've ever seen him.

"Tell me you don't want to talk to me and I'll go," he says. "But if it's just because you're afraid of my dad, then forget it."

"I'm not *afraid* of your dad. I just . . . I'm afraid . . ." *I'm afraid for* you, I don't say. He doesn't want to hear it. I return my attention to the card game, lay off a few, discard. "I'll never forgive myself for what he did to you."

Max scoffs. "Pretty self-centered of you to think it was your fault."

"It *was* my fault."

"No. And you know what? It wasn't mine either. He's the grown-ass man who lost his temper. He's the one who decided he was done talking."

I bite my tongue. Shake my head. I don't want to argue with him. Yeah, sure, it's Mr. Palazzola's fault, but that doesn't mean I carry no blame.

Max only tolerates my silence for a short moment before he says, "Stop that."

My eyes snap to him. This close, it's easy to see how much he's really changed. How his face has slimmed, his cheekbones more prominent. The freckles across his nose have faded, barely there if you know where to look. His clothes fit him now. Both of us grew up in pants that were too short for us, sleeves that just reached the bones of our wrists.

What else about him has changed?

"I know what you're thinking," he adds.

"No, you don't."

"I know *you*, Nat. And you said it yourself. You haven't changed. So I still know you." He discards the last of his hand, leaving me with three in mine. He doesn't bother counting points. Just gathers up the cards and shuffles.

He's right. He does know me. Better than I do, with how detached I feel from myself most of the time.

And that's dangerous. He could unravel everything I've tried to make of myself. This is a thread that should not be tugged. A relationship that needs to stay boxed up in the past, locked away in inaccessible memories.

But when he deals another round, I take up my hand and play our game.

Silence stretches between us as we lay out our cards, turn after turn. We never had many quiet moments together back then. Always on the move, we were. Always seeking out the next thrill. Quiet was reserved for mourning, when we could offer nothing more than our presence and a shoulder to lean on.

When my hamster, Egg, got out of her cage in the night and we never saw her again.

When Max lost his mom to illness in ninth grade.

When we lost each other.

This shouldn't be a time of mourning.

"It's been hard without you." I don't mean to sound so broken when I say it. He doesn't need a guilt trip.

"Dude, same."

I breathe out a shaky laugh, and for a second, it's like no time has passed at all. Max and I are fifteen years old, playing a game of Rummy in the sunroom at my house, sharing stolen bags of chips and tall cans of Labatt Blue while my parents are out for the night.

We're kids who will keep doing whatever they want and will never know consequence.

A loud burst of laughter from the dining hall breaks the spell. Max and I are eighteen, college freshmen, and if we tried pulling the shit we used to do now, we'd end up in prison. Now, we have GPAs to worry about, and he's got lacrosse, and the future doesn't feel so far away and indestructible.

I slip a card into my sleeve for later, lay off a run, discard.

"What about you?" I say. "Have you changed?"

Max smiles. All in the eyes. "See for yourself."

I smile back.

I wonder what our friendship will look like without the undercurrent of crime and chaos. It won't be the same. Not even close.

Maybe . . . maybe it will be better.

CHAPTER 13

MICKEY IS GRUMPY NEXT time I see him. *Actually* grumpy, not his usual stoicism. Chin in hands, lips pursed, eyebrows angry, staring straight ahead at the board as I walk into public speaking Tuesday morning.

Celeste sits next to him, also with her chin in her hands, leaning in and talking Mickey's ear off with this absolute shit-eating grin on her face.

I hesitate in the doorway. If Max and I are going to be all right, I can talk to her again, yeah? Or maybe she was put off by my dramatics at the Throne Room.

She catches my eye as I'm busy debating what to do. Motions to the empty seat beside her with a jut of her chin. The tension melts out of my body with a sigh of relief as I slink over to their table and slump into my chair.

"Hey."

"Hey there," Celeste says.

"Friends again?"

She raises an eyebrow. "Were we ever?"

I let out a breathy chuckle, and the only way I can describe Celeste's smile then is *fond*. She turns back to continue tormenting Mickey.

"He's taller than you, isn't he?" she says. "That's where the issue lies."

Mickey snatches up his plastic coffee cup and swirls it rather aggressively before taking a sip through the straw. "There is no issue."

"The look on your face says there is a *major* issue."

I lean over to fish my notebook out of my backpack on the floor.

"Well, it's not what you think it is," Mickey argues.

"So enlighten me."

I slap the notebook on the table and flip page by page until I get to the sloppy and minimal notes I took last time I managed to make it to class.

"How about not in the middle of class," Mickey says.

Celeste heaves a sigh. "Fiiiine."

On the next page after my class notes is a list of potential opening lines for my personal narrative. Professor Huang says the first line has to be just as gripping as if we were writing a novel. Grab the audience's attention, make them want to keep listening even when you're just some random college kid no one actually wants to hear speak.

Most of the openers I have listed boast about my ability to get away with things. The number of crimes I've committed against the number of times I've been caught. Others try to capture the rush of it all.

It's edgy and annoying in a way that churns my stomach.

But the last one . . .

There's no way I wrote the last one. It's barely legible, scribbled at a harsh angle, small letters overlapping each other, drifting into the line beneath it.

I think I prefer it when I'm dissociating because when I'm fully here, fully present in my mind, I start to realize I don't like myself very much.

I read over it again and again, a frown etching deeper with each pass, until I put my elbows on the table and press my palms into my eyes.

No way I was *fully present in my mind* when I wrote this. It must've been during those days I locked myself away doing homework and pushed myself into a dissociative break.

I don't like myself very much.

"I'm glad you and Max are talking," Celeste is saying. I drop my arms over the page to hide my words from both of us and turn to face her as she adds, "It's been boring without you."

I push the corner of my mouth up into a smirk. "And yet we're not friends."

"Seems to be a theme for her," Mickey mutters into his coffee.

I laugh. I smile. I make jokes. I pretend, until Professor Huang shows up and puts us to work.

But my head keeps going back to those words in my own writing that I should never have put to paper and made real.

I don't like myself very much.

Might be the most honest I've ever been.

AFTER I GOT KICKED off the lacrosse team, I shoved my gear in the way back of the closet I shared with my brother and never touched it again. This is the first time I've held a stick in almost two years.

Saying I've missed it would be a gross understatement. I built so much of myself around this sport that when I lost it, any sense of self I'd managed to hold on to without Max around slipped away with it.

I was on probation, banned from more stores than I was allowed in, with nothing to put my energy toward. I had no friends. And I couldn't play lacrosse. All I had was myself and my cards and foam swords.

Taking the spare stick Celeste offers me in the field house that afternoon feels like it should be accompanied by a beam of radiant light pouring down over me. Some kind of epic ballad playing in the background—a song fit for the anti-hero's moment of true redemption.

But Celeste just hands it over and scoops a ball up in her own net without feeling the significance of it.

I curl my fingers loosely around the shaft. Give the stick a spin.

The field house smells like rubber and floor polish. Royals basketball and volleyball championship banners hang from the rafters, the purple washed out by the harsh fluorescent lights buzzing high overhead.

It's also where the lacrosse teams practice in the pre-season, when the field outside is buried under snow and no amount of physical activity can ward off the cold. Where I'd spend most of my time if I'd made it this far.

"Nathaniel."

I look up when Tasha calls my name, poised to send me a pass. I catch it with ease, even with the shallower pocket of the women's stick, the weight of it bringing me right back to sophomore year, before I lost Max and the game, when everything looked so promising and I could do anything. I smile as I twirl the stick, cradle the ball a few times to get a feel for the pocket.

"You feeling better?" Tasha asks as they catch my return pass.

"Yeah," I say, and I really mean it. Even with those notes

I found earlier, I feel pretty good now. Cautiously optimistic. "Sorry I kind of just . . . shut down the other day."

"It's okay," Tasha says at the same time Celeste plants the butt of her stick on the floor and says, "You can talk to us about things, you know. Instead of shutting down."

Tasha sends the ball back to me and I cradle it by my ear, looking at Celeste until she gets her stick ready.

"Only if you admit we're friends," I say.

She lets the ball hit her pocket and bounce back out, scowling at me. "I would rather die."

I press a hand over my heart and wince theatrically. "*Oof, ouch.*"

She grins and scoops up the ball, snaps it over to Tasha, who lines up a pass to me. It's arching right to my pocket when Celeste jumps in to intercept it, and it becomes a game of Keep Away, with the two of them passing long and high and me in the middle trying to get it back.

It's more fun than jumping out of that window, or crashing parties, or having people sneer at me. Might even be more fun than thievery.

I started playing lacrosse way back in elementary school, when my family was still a family and Mom and Dad took Seth and me to Buffalo Bandits games because they were way cheaper than Sabres or Bills games. It was exhilarating, with the music and the funny announcements even during gameplay. Like the crowd was part of the game.

Field lacrosse might be a whole different game from box lacrosse, but I threw myself into it all the same. I like to think my stick skills and sword skills benefited from each other too.

I finally manage to get the ball back when Tasha lobs it high overhead. I jump, stretching my arm and stick out as far as they'll go, using my longer reach to steal it from over Celeste's head. I'm out of breath and laughing, bent over with the stick across my thighs to hold me up, when the door swings open.

Max steps in, a field stick propped against his shoulder.

The sight of him instantly puts me back on the defensive. I stand up straight, tighten my grip around my borrowed stick, fight the urge to drop it and walk away. It's going to take a while to get used to having him around again.

Celeste shrugs when I give her a look. "What? You said we should get to know him."

Max drops his backpack to the floor and lifts his stick all in one smooth motion, calling for the ball. Tasha scoops it up and tosses it toward him. He catches it one-handed, crosses it over his body to get a two-hand hold on it, and passes to Celeste.

The energy has pretty much evaporated now. I keep my eyes on the ball as it makes its way around the circle again, all the chaos of Keep Away lost to the rigidity of one expected pass after the other. Everyone is quiet, like they're trying to figure out this new dynamic and adapt to it before opening their mouths and risking this tentative peace.

I almost drop a few passes because I'm so tense, I forget to give with it. It only makes it worse. I've talked myself up like some kind of lacrosse star, and women's stick or not, right now I look shaky at best.

The silence drags on for a few minutes before Celeste breaks it with a deadpan, "This is a riveting conversation, truly."

Tasha lets out a strained laugh, catching the ball right-handed and passing it to Max with their left. He catches it and stops, holding his stick across his hips.

"I don't hear you saying anything," he says.

"Did I not just speak?"

"Ah, yes, pointing out the lack of conversation, hoping someone else will do the actual work to make it instead of saying something of substance."

I look back and forth between them, the back of my neck prickling. Tasha said he's mostly kept to himself, so I don't know how Celeste will take having her snark aimed back at her from someone she doesn't really know.

There's one thing about Max that hasn't changed, I suppose. He makes compliments sound like insults, comfort sting like barbed wire, and he's never been afraid to call someone on their shit.

Celeste cocks her head to the side, mouth twitching against either a sneer or a smile. I look at Tasha, who meets my gaze with wide eyes, tugging nervously on their shooting strings.

And then Celeste laughs. A single burst of sound, followed up with a toothy grin. "Fine. A conversation starter then. How did the two of you meet and start doing crimes together?"

I grimace, giving Max a sidelong glance. I've already given up enough of his history. He can take the lead on this.

Except he looks at me, eyes crinkled in a smile. "Why don't you tell 'em, Nat?"

He looks far too amused for this to be a malicious thing, but it definitely feels like he's challenging me somehow. Like he wants to see how honest I am these days.

If I were to tell this story like it were about anyone other than him, I'd spin it into something more outlandish, play it up like some kind of big-screen moment instead of the embarrassment that it was.

But because it's about Max, I can only tell the truth.

"I tried to pickpocket him. He caught me."

"And a beautiful friendship was born," he adds dryly.

"Okay, I'll be the one to say it this time." Tasha uses their stick for leverage as they lower themself to the green rubber flooring, sitting cross-legged. "Details, please."

Max hums, holding his stick in one hand and bouncing the ball to himself once before plopping down to the ground. He pats the space beside him and grins. "Story time."

We sit in a circle together, close enough that our knees almost touch. I keep my head down, tugging on the strings of my stick to adjust the pocket before remembering it's not mine to be messing with. I rest it across my lap, put my elbows on my knees and chin in my hands, and look at Max as expectantly as the others.

"Don't look at me." He jerks his chin toward me. "This is Nat's story to start."

All eyes focus on me. I purse my lips. Part of me wants to bask in the attention, lean back with my elbows propping me up and my ankles crossed and a smirk on my face. Another part of me wants to shrink so fully into myself that I compact into a single, imperceptible atom. I don't know who I'm supposed to be in this situation.

Max's Nat, or Hartland's obnoxious e-boy, Nathaniel.

"Well . . . ," I start slowly, tapping my fingers along my cheekbones. "I'd been playing a lot of *Skyrim* at the time."

The disbelieving sound Celeste makes is so loud it startles me. For a second I'm afraid she might be choking. "Do not even say your criminal habits were inspired by video games. Don't give boomers the satisfaction."

Max snickers, drawing a grin out of me. "Nah, the problem

is that *Skyrim* never showed the actual act of pickpocketing," I say. "Just the inventory screen, y'know? So I went looking for tutorials because I didn't get how anyone could just stick their hand in someone's pocket without being noticed. Really, if Bethesda had been more detailed in their crime mechanics, curiosity wouldn't've gotten the better of me."

"Riiiight," Celeste says.

Max leans in, eyes alight. "Yeah, so it's my first day at this new school, it's, like, sixth grade, I'm in the lunch line and I feel someone just . . . jam their fingers right into my back pocket. No dexterity at all, just . . ." He makes a circle with the fingers of his left hand and shoves the other through it almost violently.

"Oh come on." I reach over to push his hands down, stop him from making that motion repeatedly, and snatch my hand back as soon as I realize what I'm doing. We're not at that level of comfort anymore. "Only reason you noticed was because that fuckin' . . . football love note got caught on the tear in your pocket."

Max snorts and Tasha says, "Football love note?"

He makes a triangle with his thumbs and forefingers. "Yeah, you know those notes folded up in a triangle, you shoot them through your friends' fingers like a field goal? Open it up and find, *Do you like me? Circle yes or no.*"

"Ah, so new boy catching eyes and collecting love

confessions on day one, huh?" Celeste says. "I'm a bit impressed."

I shake my head and cluck my tongue. "Don't be. We never got new kids. Max was all fresh and exciting. Nothing to do with his face."

Max nods sagely. "It's true. I was one ugly kid."

Celeste motions for us to move on. "Okay, so you catch him with his hand in your pocket. Then what?"

Max shrugs. "I punched him in the face and started a lunchroom brawl."

Celeste narrows her eyes, entirely unconvinced. Max seems content to leave it at that, rolling the lacrosse ball from hand to hand on the floor, smiling like he's reminiscing. But I can't stand for anyone to see him as less perfect than he is.

I snatch the ball as it rolls between his hands. "He offered to pay for my lunch."

"My mom gave me a nice, crisp ten-dollar bill that morning," he says. "I was feeling charitable."

He's always done this. Downplayed every good thing he's ever done for another person. Sometimes I wonder if that's my fault too. If I let him take the fall so many times, he's convinced himself he's not actually a good person at all.

"Wow, you're a real treasure, aren't you?" Celeste drawls.

When Max snorts a laugh, my face feels unreasonably warm.

Celeste leans back on her hands, ankles crossed in front of her as she cocks her head to the side and eyes Max. "You're majoring in forensics, right? How do you go from crime to that?"

I screw my face up at Max, confused. "Forensics? Since when?"

He shrugs lazily. "Dad kept me on a short leash after we moved, could only really leave the house for school and lacrosse, so I was stuck with him watching all his true crime documentaries. Then forensics was a senior year elective and I thought it'd be fun, and well, it was."

Max snatches the ball back from me and bounces it beside his knee. "Enough about me and Nat. What about the two of you?" he asks. "I remember the first party at the lax house in the fall, you two were already pretty close, yeah?"

"Yeah," Tasha agrees, twisting to stretch their back. "We met as prospies last year and stayed in touch through the summer."

Celeste nods her affirmation. "My older brother told me college is the last time it's easy to make friends, then adulthood comes around and everyone forgets how. So when I found out Tasha's into all the same nerdy shit as me, I latched on to them."

Max quirks an eyebrow. "Nerdy shit?" A second later, he snaps his fingers. "Oh! You cosplay, right?"

"Yeah, and they do really good fantasy photography."

"Shit, hey." Max smacks my knee with the back of his hand and I blink in surprise. "You shown them your sword collection?"

My face is still burning up, like I'm coming down with a fever or something. I scuff the heel of my shoe against the rubber floor, looking down so they can't see if I'm all red or not. "Yeah, we've already talked about taking some pictures with them." He gives me a look that says *Uhhh, what about me?* and I can't stop myself from smiling even as I roll my eyes. "Didn't we just get done talking about how ugly you are? You'd ruin the vibe."

"No way. I can be a lowly background peasant to bring more life to the scene, while you, like, get stepped on by some badass fantasy lady for thinking you could challenge her."

"Ahem?" Celeste leans in, raising a hand. "And I'm the badass lady that gets to step on him, right?"

"No shit."

"Well damn, I'm happy to do that anytime."

Tasha snickers, folding their hands under their chin with an uncharacteristically devious grin. "Oh, this will be fun."

The three of them start putting together a whole

backstory for these characters, even Max's peasant, and as I sit watching my old world and my new come together so seamlessly, I feel . . .

I sigh, letting my head roll to the side.

I feel content.

CHAPTER 14

THANKFULLY, THEY DECIDE TO spare me the frostbite, planning the photoshoot for later in the semester when the snow melts a bit. But Celeste and Max are taking this whole thing extremely seriously. The four of us spend Wednesday afternoon in the library study cubby, but instead of doing homework, Max is planning out costume ideas with Celeste, joking around with her in that dry manner they share like *they're* the childhood friends here.

I'm half-jealous and half-hopeful, like maybe they'll become better friends with each other than they are with me, but also maybe like I've finally found my people. Like Celeste's brother told her, this is the time to forge lasting friendships, right?

I chew on a pen cap in an attempt to hide my smile as I watch, but judging by the way Tasha throws a Swedish Fish at me and sticks out their tongue when I look over, it doesn't work at all. I reach over to clasp my hand around their forearm in a *yeah you caught me* kinda way.

A minute later, I realize I haven't let go, and Tasha hasn't stopped smiling.

I don't immediately snatch my hand away, which I guess is progress. Instead, I let my hand fall more casually onto the armrest we share, still brushing their skin.

After the library, we take a drive up to a craft store in Auburn for Celeste to buy materials for the fantasy costumes and our Erotic Ball outfits. Celeste has an old sedan handed down to her by her brother, a teal rosary draped over the rearview mirror and a dried rose sticking out of one of the vents.

Celeste plays a mix of Stray Kids, Lil Nas X, and Bad Bunny, and she and Tasha sing along from the front seat while Max and I laugh at them in the back. I relax into the headrest and close my eyes, listening to their voices mingle.

This must have been what it was like for those normal friend groups in high school. My brother probably drove around like this with his friends, going to stores with no intention of committing a crime, laughing and singing and simply enjoying each other's company no matter how boring those people were.

The thought inspires me to take out my phone. Snap a vague picture that shows I'm in a car with people, Tasha's hand uplifted to support the power of their vocals, Celeste's on the wheel, Max's reaching forward to sneak Celeste's phone from the center console to change the song.

I send it to my brother. Another contextless picture in our back-and-forth. I don't know if it's to prove that I'm capable of making friends or . . . or maybe because being around people and feeling at ease gives me a shred of hope that it might not be too late for us.

Not forcing it. Never forcing it. But it wouldn't hurt to try to be friends.

If he and I start talking every once in a while, it'll get back to my parents, and maybe they won't see me as such a lost cause anymore.

He hasn't responded by the time we get to the craft store, but it's not enough to bother me in this company.

Several heads swivel in our direction as we step inside, not loud with our voices, but loud in our presence. Max's height. Celeste's confidence. The way Tasha and I are dressed. Today I've got on this rough denim jacket, an oversized black T-shirt that says *Guess I'll die* in some funky nineties bubble font tucked into black chinos and rolled above my ankles to give a glimpse of high, electric blue socks in black-and-white checkered Vans. A single chain hangs from my belt loops. Most people turn away after getting a quick look at us, while others let their stares linger. I slouch my shoulders and try to carry myself naturally. No pinned-on smirks or false airs.

But that just makes me overly conscious of my body and how it moves, the way I'm holding my face, and it's so distracting that it makes me feel fuzzy.

Seems I can't win.

Celeste and Max get right to work, sorting through fabric samples and sewing patterns, both of them looking as focused as they do on the lacrosse field. Like I said, they're taking this photoshoot thing seriously.

I suppose that's one way Max has changed. He would listen and nod along and ask questions when I went on my tangents about superior video game swords and he'd swing them around with me whenever I brought them out, but I never got the impression that he'd actually be into them without my influence. Never would've guessed he'd be this into cosplay either. He's always been the more textbook jock of the two of us.

Unless I just wasn't paying enough attention, too wrapped up in my own head and my own issues to really know my own best friend.

I don't realize I'm zoned out and frowning until Tasha nudges me with an elbow. I blink my way out of my head and force a smile. "What's up?"

"You all right?"

"Oh, yeah, totally. Just zoned for a second there."

I'm starting to recognize that little smile of theirs. The one they get when they think they can see right through me, and whatever they find makes them sad.

"Want to look for things for the dance? I think those two are gonna be a while."

I nod and follow them a few aisles away, where there's gaudier fabrics better suited for *Things That Go Bump in the Night* on display. They rub a square of black felt between their fingers, but they're still giving me that soul-searching look.

If I wasn't feeling so off-balance, I'd put my hands in my pockets and lean in, eyebrows raised and eyes wide to give them a better look. Now, I can't hold up to it. I turn to the racks of fabric and run my hand along the different textures.

"What?"

They cock their head to the side curiously. "You just seem . . . I don't know." They shake their head and turn their attention to the satin. "I'm glad things didn't stay weird between us for long."

"There was no reason for them to, right?" I try for a light and easy grin. I think it's convincing enough, judging by the way they glance at me and ease up a bit, their smile softening.

"Right." They meander through the racks, and I trail after them, feeling each different sample. "You still planning on going all vampy?"

"Ah, yeah. It might not be the most original, but I think it suits me."

"It does. And with you and Celeste combining your talents, I'm sure you'll stand out."

"Max too, apparently," I mutter.

"Apparently?"

I shake my head dismissively. "I'm just surprised he's getting so into this. He's always been all about facts and science. He was never into the fantasy stuff the way I was."

"Well, maybe he's just excited to have you back, so he wants to be as involved as possible in what you've got going on, you know?"

I frown. "I don't want him just . . . following my lead. The way he did before."

That'll undoubtedly lead him right back into trouble.

Tasha pulls down a swath of black satin, letting it ripple toward the floor. "I don't think you're giving him enough credit. He seems plenty sure of who he is without your lead. And I bet"—they turn to me as they drape the fabric over their shoulder like a sash—"he knew back then too."

They tilt their chin up, lips quirked in self-satisfaction, and start marching back toward the others. The satin they carry breezes against the back of my hand.

I close my eyes and breathe in slowly through my nose.

Maybe they're right. If I don't even know myself, how can I stand here and claim to know a single thing about Max?

CHAPTER 15

IT STILL JUMP SCARES me a little when Max's name shows up on my phone.

We go from over two years of no contact to meals together a few times a week, occasional study sessions in the library, and texts while he's on the bus ride back from an away game like:

Max
Totally annihilated them
Party at the lax house

See, if it were an ordinary dorm party, or at one of the other off-campus houses, maybe I'd be quicker to jump on it. Quicker to fall into the role I've made for myself as a party-crashing nuisance, no worries that it's a Tuesday night.

But the lax house? With all his teammates, people who know him apart from me? People doing with their lives the one thing I wanted, that I ruined for myself? No way.

So I send back:

Sweet man have fun

Max
That was an invitation nat
Tasha and celeste will be there too

I get ready with shaking hands. It's a relief I'm not having to tone myself down after all, no reason to stay under the radar. My style is the one honest thing about me, the one thing that doesn't feel like acting.

Tasha comes down an hour later, camera bag in tow and a broad smile on their face. "This is a big win," they say, bouncing on their toes.

"Tuesday night rager? Must've been."

"The captains on both teams are part of USA Lacrosse together," they explain. "We, or well, the men's team, haven't beat them since they were all freshmen. Big rivalry there."

We meet up with Celeste and some of the others from the women's team on the way off campus, already drinking from giant water bottles covered in stickers. I feel out of place among their laughter and general joy.

This is what I wanted for myself. I never wanted to be in college without the lacrosse backdrop. I'm living a watered-down version of the life I'd always pictured for myself at this age.

It'll be worse when I'm with Max and his team too. I've

never been around him and his other friends at the same time. What if having me and them together in the same place makes it painfully clear to him how inferior I am?

Max was always better with people than me. He's the kind of person that can blend in with any group, get along with anyone, even if they have nothing in common with him. I was just the weirdo in his shadow at school, only stepping out of it when we were alone. That's when I took the lead, right into trouble.

Sometimes I think he only stayed friends with me because he felt bad. Tasha was right—he did always know who he was. Too good to leave the toxic friend behind even when it would've been so much better for him.

Celeste sidling up to me breaks me out of my thoughts. "Brooding doesn't suit you. E-boys are supposed to be more smirky."

I shake my head, brush some hair out of my face. "I wasn't brooding. I was smoldering."

She full-body grimaces. "Yeesh. Poorly done."

"You think you could do better?"

"I could, but I'm not showing you." She turns her nose up at me. "I save my smolder for the worthy."

"Damn. Something for me to aspire to then."

Celeste's smile is fully smug. She got what she wanted, and my nerves aren't firing so out of control now. Tasha hooks their arm into mine. "I'll stick with you if you want," they say. "I bet the boys'll be a bit rowdy."

A bit rowdy is an understatement. We can hear their music and shouting from a block away, and as soon as we step into the house, the absolute chaos shunts me halfway out of my body. The whole men's team is packed into the living room right where we enter, barking a Royals victory chant together. The two guys leading the chant from the center of the huddle must be the captains. Max is to the left, surrounded on all sides by his new teammates, red in the face as he yells along with them.

Tasha takes shots of the whole thing. They look like movie stills from what I can see over their shoulder, every one of the guys getting a chance to be the main character. We circle around to the other side of the room by the time they finish off with one final roar of pride. The house erupts into even louder cheering, clapping, whistling. The energy gets my heart racing, and I don't think it's going to come down for the rest of the night.

I can imagine myself in that huddle, riding the adrenaline of a hard-fought victory. My chest aches with longing. I want this. I want to belong to it. Not even my high school team had this kind of bond, at least not that I ever got to be a part of. They tolerated me for my assist records, my willingness to forgo a flashy play for myself if it meant passing off for a sure goal. I could've set up every single game-winning goal, put my own face in the mud for it, but since I wasn't the one taking the shot, I wasn't the one being swarmed for the celly. My coaches were the only ones who ever acknowledged my part in anything.

But these guys? These guys seem like they value teamwork over the name attached to a goal. I could have been a part of this if I hadn't blown everything apart.

Max doesn't immediately seek me out once things have calmed down to a normal level of house party commotion. That's fine by me. I'm glad to catch glimpses of him laughing with his team while Tasha keeps their hand in mine unless it's on the shutter of their camera.

I'm surprised the constant contact doesn't get anxiety boiling through me. Instead, I miss it when they're taking pictures. Even move my hand to meet theirs when they offer it back to me. It makes me feel like I belong here, among these teams and their friends. I'm not crashing this party. I don't need to make a spectacle of myself. I can just be.

There's beer pong in the kitchen, King's Cup in the sunken den, and circles of people crowding every square inch of the house, and not once do I get the out-of-place feeling I had on the way here. Celeste stays with Tasha and me unless she's ducking into the kitchen for a shot, and they're the ones to introduce me to people.

When they show me to their captain, Bailey James, she

puts a hand on my shoulder, the other holding an empty wine cooler. She's listing to the side as she practically yells at me, "Hey, it's you! My brother told me about you!"

I make a show of looking side to side and going, "Uhh . . ."

She throws her head back and laughs. "Nothing too bad, don't worry! I'm glad he's making friends who don't know shit about hockey!"

She gets pulled away by a couple of the girls, but I'm left feeling warm, maybe even smiley. Mickey thinks of me as a friend? At least, he talks about me in a way that makes other people think that.

Max comes around close to an hour after we show up, flushed but coherent as he says, "Sorry, had my first start today so the boys won't let me know peace."

Celeste almost chokes on her drink. "Wait, *you* played this game? They put their freshman goalie in for a rivalry matchup?"

"Hey, clearly it worked!" Tasha says. They raise a hand for a high five that Max accepts so eagerly, I can hear the slap over the cacophony of the party. Tasha laughs through an *ow!*, shaking out their hand.

Max grins sheepishly. "Sorry, got a little too excited." He looks to me next. "I told Coach about your sophomore year assist record, by the way."

I *was* smiling, but at that, I feel my eyes bug out of my face. "You what?"

"Yeah, he might shoot you an email or something. Not till the end of the season, though, so don't go refreshing your inbox."

My mouth is hanging open when Max gets whisked away again, this time for a celebratory beer bong. I watch him go. I wonder if this was what it was like for him in high school, when he went out without me. If he was a precious commodity all those nights like he is now, all his other friends ecstatic for the times he could get away from me.

It wasn't that he kept me separate from them on purpose, because he was embarrassed of me or anything. I did it to myself.

Now here we are, me and my friends, Max and his, us.

And it might not be too late for me to be a part of this.

I look around at the crowd like I'm seeing them for the first time. Could these really be my teammates next year? I'll need to start conditioning, rebuilding my skill set.

Tasha squeezes my hand. "Nathaniel! That's exciting!"

I clench my jaw shut and shake my head, swallowing hard. "I haven't played in so long, I doubt they'll pick me up that easy."

Celeste tilts the mouth of her beer bottle toward me. "None of that self-defeating nonsense tonight. We're partying."

"*You're* partying."

"Wanna do a shot with me?" she counters.

I've never been a drinker, but right now? Right now, I feel like a shot.

The three of us push our way into the kitchen, where a girl pours each of us a shot of a bright blue liquor. We clink our glasses together and down them to the sounds of whooping and cheering. It burns down my throat, taking the worry of what might happen next year with it.

We settle down in the den after that, where King's Cup is still going strong. We take a spot squished together on the floor to join in, but as soon as we sit, one of the guys shouts, "The e-boy! I've been waiting for you to show up at one of these parties."

My smirk comes loose and easy, aided by the liquor. "Didn't realize I was in such high demand."

"You do magic tricks, right?" He folds forward and gathers up a messy handful of cards from the table, his movements jerky from the alcohol.

"You gotta do everything you just pulled now, man!" another player says.

The first guy waves him off. "We play King's all the time. How often do we get our own magic show?" He holds the cards out to me, spilling half of them over the table.

I reach into my pocket and pull out my showy crystal-themed cardistry deck. "I can do you one better," I say, fanning them out to show off the way the light glints off the metallic colors.

Tasha bounces on their heels next to me, getting their camera ready. "I've been dying for a real show of this too."

Max isn't here with me now. I'm surrounded by lacrosse players. But flourishing my cards to genuine astonishment makes me feel right at home. I even break out into some of the card magic they were expecting—things I don't have as much practice with because they require another person.

The way they eat it up, I think I have an idea of what it feels like to belong.

CHAPTER 16

I DON'T NEED ALL of campus to see me anymore. I have my friends. And when I don't have them, because they're at practice or away games, or bogged down with homework, I don't go looking for outside attention.

Instead, I take the spare lacrosse stick Max loans me up to the field house and do some wall ball. Start up a gym routine to ease myself back into physical exertion.

Next year, I will be on that field in a Royals uniform. No matter what it takes.

I have a real, tangible thing to work toward.

These few weeks that pass are some of the best I've had in years. So much so that the anxiety of Erotic Ball doesn't catch up with me until the day of.

I've never been to a school dance. Never had a date, and Max always did, so I stayed home rather than get in his way.

He tried to convince me to ask someone in the weeks leading up to every dance. Gave me names of people he supposedly knew were interested. I even got asked directly by this girl from my tenth grade social studies class, but I'm pretty sure that was a joke. She seemed pretty offended when I said no.

The closest I ever got to the pageantry of it all was sitting on the porch steps, watching my brother pose with his girlfriend, Riley, and all their friends before homecomings and proms. It was always our house they congregated at, even with its tiny size, because our parents loved having well-behaved teenagers around. We hosted all their movie nights and bonfires and cookouts, and I always watched from the periphery, never invited to join.

Because I am not a well-behaved teenager.

They'd kick me off the steps eventually to get more creative with their posing, and I'd go to my room, silently close the door, and lay in my bunk wondering why the fuck I am the way I am.

I know why.

I know exactly why.

Why I couldn't hook up with Tasha, why I couldn't bring myself to date anyone in high school, why I barely remember most of my childhood.

Why my mind detaches from my body whenever I start to feel too much.

But just because I know it doesn't mean I will ever acknowledge it.

Seth and Riley started dating their freshman year of high school and got married a month after graduation, because that's what guys who build their whole personalities off their military aspirations do. My sister-in-law was always nice to me when she came over to the house. Refused to even look at me at school, when her friends were around. I don't think I can blame her, though. Not anymore. If I'm over here writing theses on how much I hate myself, I can't go around expecting anyone else to feel differently.

Watching my brother and his friends get ready for dances was never like this, with Celeste's music blasting from her phone in my dorm room as she covers me in special FX makeup to make me look like I've been gnawed on and Max and Tasha getting changed with their backs to us, barely trying to cover their skin.

No, Seth and his friends were clean-cut and well put together on a normal day. For dances, they put on full suits and floor-length gowns, or two-pieces with rhinestone crop tops and high-waisted, billowing skirts. One of his friends even wore a cummerbund to senior prom.

I guess it's only fitting that my first ever dance experience is a school-sanctioned precursor to an orgy.

Fitting in a way that makes Max stop me outside the door to the student union, nodding for Tasha and Celeste to go on ahead of us. The doors are propped open, sending flashing lights, artificial mist, and bassy music wafting out into the otherwise calm night.

"You gonna be okay with this?" he asks me. He's dressed in these tight, shiny black pants, a black mesh shirt, with little fangs and a chest harness with small wings attached to the back. Some kind of demony creature. I've seen plenty of similar outfits, along with even more vampires, like me, on our way here.

I narrow my eyes at him. Am I really so unversed in school social events that he feels the need to check on me?

"Why wouldn't I be?" I say, not bothering to hold back the bite in my voice. Max doesn't even blink.

A group of totally shirtless guys in dog ear headbands and torn-up jean shorts passes between us as we stand at opposite sides of the doorway. One of them tosses a not entirely empty can down on the stairs just before stepping inside, sending a spray of beer up toward my knees. I flinch back a step.

Max clenches his jaw until they're gone, then steps closer to me so we're out of the way of others' arrival. He lowers his voice. "You've never been comfortable with this kind of shit." He motions toward my chest, exposed by a billowy satin shirt, sewn custom for me by Celeste.

It takes me a second to understand what he's getting at. The near nudity. The sexually charged nature of the whole thing.

We stand there studying each other, silent and tense.

Max doesn't know. He doesn't know, he's just making assumptions about my lack of experience. He has no idea what he's talking about.

I shake my head to snap the tension and grin with all of my teeth. "Oh, trust me, this is like my comfort zone."

He blinks slowly, unimpressed. "Is that so."

The grin falls away. He's not allowed to do this. Just come back into my life and completely nerf the persona I've put so much effort into. If I have to push my own boundaries to prove him wrong, I will.

I match his blank expression and hold eye contact as I step forward, only breaking it when I pass by him into the building. The others are waiting in the dimly lit entry hall and I don't give them time to ask questions before holding a hand out to Tasha and asking them to dance with me.

They smile. Dip their head and hold on to the crook of my elbow. They are dressed as a nymph, ethereal in their androgyny, with makeup sharpening their features and extensions in their hair slicked down to cover their chest over their pale, flesh-colored binder, along with black leather pants that lace in the front, like a pirate.

I shoot Max a backward glance. He looks unconvinced, but what the fuck does he know?

We step out of the entry hall and fully into the dance, where the only light comes from colorful strobe lights illuminating flashes of skin and too-wide drunken smiles.

In this mass of dancing bodies, I can be anyone I want to be.

I HAVEN'T HAD a sip of alcohol tonight, but I feel loose and warm like I've chugged a whole case by myself. Happy, like nothing bad has ever happened to me.

Maybe it's a contact high from the whiffs of weed I keep catching from somewhere in the crowd. Or maybe this is just how it feels to be normal for once. To spend a night with friends where the fun is all in the company you keep and not reliant on thrill-seeking and limit-pushing.

The crowd around us is really leaning into the erotic theme, grinding on each other in varying degrees of seriousness and lust, but me and Tasha hold each other and sway even when it doesn't match up with the music, or hold hands and jump around together during the super energetic songs. Eventually Celeste joins us, pressing up against Tasha's back and reaching around them to grab onto me so the three of us can all dance together.

My face hurts from how big I smile. How real it is.

Is this what high school could've been like if I'd just been more normal? Did Seth and his clean-cut friends have this much fun at their well-behaved dances and parties? When Max went to all those dances without me . . . did he feel free like this?

I glance over at him then. His head is thrown back in laughter, dancing with this guy I've never seen before. They bumped into each other in the crowd and melded together almost naturally. Their hands are clasped and raised up by their faces, until Max lets go to curl an arm around the guy's waist.

They're in their own world, and I am very much on the outside.

Of course Max felt freer at those dances. Without me there to entice him into trouble. With only his dates and their friends, he could pretend for just one night that he had an average high school life too, and didn't have a best friend sitting at home plotting his next petty crime.

Why did he even bother approaching me at the lacrosse game? Hunting me down on campus. He would've been better off letting me go.

Tasha's fingertips on my jaw snap me back to attention, and they gently turn my face toward them. "Hey," they say just loud enough to be heard over the music. "Where'd you go?"

I blink down at them, suddenly aware of how still I'm standing, how far away I was. I blink again and shake my head, pressing the heel of my free hand to my forehead. I'm sweating. I feel it drip down my temple.

Celeste leans in with her chin on Tasha's shoulder. It's hard to hear, but I think she asks Tasha if I'm okay.

Tasha shakes their head slightly, then tugs on my hand, guiding me through the crowd and out the double doors. As soon as the cold, late March air hits me, I realize how close I was to burning up. I sit down heavily on the steps and wipe my face with the loose collar of my shirt, leaving smears of makeup behind. Tasha sits beside me, giving me a couple feet of space, and Celeste leans against the stone railing, arms crossed as she locks her eyes on me with such intensity, I'm pretty sure she's trying to see through my skull, into whatever my brain matter is hiding.

I wait for them to ask the question, and they wait for me to answer it unprompted, leaving us in this bubble of quiet, the music behind us muffled by distance and the haze in my head. I wipe more sweat off my neck.

I take a moment to breathe, and the burning fades to shivering. "Think I just overheated," I say finally. "Haven't had enough water today."

Tasha stands as soon as the words leave my mouth, heading back inside and leaving me with Celeste.

She purses her lips to the side as she stares me down. I gaze back at her, keeping my face passive no matter how strange it is to see her dressed up like a . . . mermaid? Siren? She's in a shimmery teal bikini top and skintight leggings to match, shells and seaweed in her hair. Her nails are painted in shades of blue fish scales. Definitely not Slenderman. There's not a single tentacle in sight. Either way, she won't read anything off me that I don't want her to.

"They really care about you, you know," she says after a moment.

"They hardly know me," I argue, pretty much on instinct at this point.

Celeste leans forward slightly, like it'll put emphasis on her next words. "So let them know you. Let *us* know you. Try on a little honesty for once."

I scoff, turning to face forward, out toward campus and the sliver of the lake visible through the gaps between buildings and trees down the hill. "You really think, after everything I've shared with you, that I have any problem with honesty?"

"I think you have fully built yourself on lies, Nathaniel Conti."

I keep my eyes forward. Clench my jaw. Pretend I don't feel the way my pulse races or heat rises at the back of my skull.

She can chip away at me all she wants. So can Tasha, and even Max. But the reality is, no matter how much they think they might, no one wants to see the husk of a person hiding behind these walls.

Before she can say anything else, there's a rush of movement behind me and Tasha is at my side again, holding a bottle of water out to me.

"They had these on a table in there," they say, a bit out of breath. "It's pretty warm, though, sorry."

I give them a small smile as I take the bottle. "That's okay. Thank you."

From over Tasha's shoulder, Celeste looks at me, eyes serious and mouth hard. It doesn't feel right to challenge her. Not when she's just looking out for Tasha. So I let myself shrink under the weight of her stare and avoid looking at her again as I crack open the water and chug half of it in one go.

I take a moment to catch my breath. Figure out how much to give away, if anything. Let them know me. Or convince them they already do.

"Sorry for taking you away from the dance," is what I settle on.

Tasha shakes their head quickly, the extensions barely moving with the way they're almost glued down. "It's okay. It was getting stuffy in there. Sitting out here is nice."

It is nice. Nice to have a crowd and chaos at my back and peaceful quiet laid out at my feet. Tasha's kindness at my side and Celeste's stern guidance beyond that.

I take a deep breath of brisk air and let my body relax with it. Feel the stone steps, cold and damp and rough beneath me. Remember how much skin I'm showing and suddenly feel entirely too exposed. I tug at the ties on my shirt, close up the opening over my chest so tight it almost chokes me. Hold my breath so Tasha can't hear the way it wants to speed up and thin out.

This is ridiculous. I am ridiculous. I'm eighteen years old and I should not be . . . should not be like this. I should go back inside. Back to dancing with Tasha and Celeste. These people who are so set on becoming my friends when they have no reason to want to.

Maybe I should go back to my room. Let Tasha and Celeste have fun without having to worry about me and the issues I have that they will never know about.

I'm just about to stand and make my excuses when Max calls out from behind us, "Moved the party outside and didn't invite me?"

He steps between me and Tasha and sits on one of the steps below us. Celeste pushes off the railing to join our little group in taking up the whole set of stairs.

"You were pretty caught up with that mystery guy," she says.

I squeeze my water bottle so tight the plastic crackles.

"Mystery guy's name is Jisung, thank you." Max heaves an exaggerated sigh. "And he was stolen away from me by the hockey team."

Celeste slaps her own knee, then points in Max's face. "That's who he was!"

Max raises an eyebrow in a mimicry of Celeste's typical *tell me more* face. "Is that so?"

"Oh, I can't wait to give Terzo shit for this." She looks back toward the building as she says it, downright longingly.

"Terzo? That man is in there fighting for his life as we speak. He's got, like, six hot men dancing on him. He needs rescuing, not shit."

Celeste's eyes go wide with this malicious kind of joy, like she's two seconds from throwing herself back inside to witness this.

Tasha pokes me in the shoulder, drawing my attention and giving me a questioning look. I smile, nod, and take a sip of water.

In the end, Celeste shakes her head and turns back to us. "This company will do."

The four of us sit on those steps as the dance wears on behind us, talking about nothing in particular, until the warmth of the dance wears off and the cold seeps in. A few groups have filtered out from behind us by then. We press ourselves against the railings to take up as little space as possible as they pass through us.

How are nights like this supposed to end?

After the dances Seth went to, his friends would all come back to our house for the night. Even the dates. Mom and Dad trusted them enough not to get nasty together in the living room, and Seth and I shared a bunk bed, so he couldn't exactly sneak Riley back to his room.

Judging by the looks some of them gave each other around the coffee table covered in Dad's best bacon and pancakes breakfast in the morning, I don't think that stopped them.

Max never told me what happened with his dates afterward, and I tried my best not to think about it. I didn't need another reminder of how much I was missing out on.

Tonight, he leaves with me, Celeste, and Tasha. I take a direct route back to my room, and they all follow. Celeste goes up to Tasha's room with them to change out of their costumes, with promises to be down with drinks and snacks in a few minutes, leaving me alone with Max in my empty room.

This is entirely too much. It was always just me and Max, until it was just me. Now I have him here with me again, and two others quickly cementing their place in my life, and I don't know what I'm supposed to do with myself.

I stand next to my bed, tugging at the ties on my costume shirt and chewing on my lip and staring at the wall when I catch movement out of the corner of my eye. I glance over to find Max leaning against my dresser with his arms crossed and that stupid eyebrow raise going on.

I scowl, turning away to undo the ties. "Stop that," I mutter.

"Stop what?" Max says, completely unphased.

"Looking at me like you know what I'm thinking."

"Don't I?"

I yank the shirt over my head and toss it on the floor, realize my mistake when I remember I picked up all my dirty clothes when everyone came over earlier. I scoop the shirt back up, let it drape over my forearm, clutch it to my chest as I face Max again, looking pointedly at the dresser. He keeps his eyes on my face as he opens the middle drawer—the same drawer I kept T-shirts in back home—and finally looks away to dig for one with sleeves.

He knows me too well.

"Why are you here?" I almost whisper. The building is too quiet with most people still at the dance, or on their way to afterparties at the off-campus houses. Even with the door closed, in this old, drafty building, I'm afraid if I talk too loudly now, the whole world will hear.

"We're having a movie night," Max says matter-of-factly. He pulls out a faded and worn *Rams Lacrosse* shirt. It says *Natty Con* on the back. It's what they called me when I was still in middle school, playing on a team with a bunch of juniors and seniors. Sometimes they'd call me Bratty Natty if I got too ambitious and started taking field time from them.

"Isn't your team having an afterparty or something?" I argue. "You should be there."

"We have a game on Sunday. Forty-eight-hour rule." He pushes away from the dresser, taking a couple steps toward me before holding out the shirt. "And even if we didn't, I'd be here, or you'd be there. We have lost time to make up for, Nat."

I take the shirt from him with an unsteady hand. The fabric is soft and fragile from age and too many washes. I lived in it, back then. So proud to make varsity so young. Proud to have a team nickname. Proud to have something to show off.

Max turns his back to let me change in privacy, digging in his bag for his own change of clothes. I need a shower, honestly, with the tacky feeling of old sweat on my skin, the makeup smeared on my face and neck. But it's one night, and Celeste and Tasha will be here soon.

This shirt engulfed me back in seventh grade. Now, it's a perfect fit. I wish it had a little more length to the sleeves so I could ball the excess in my hands. Instead, I'm left tugging them anxiously to the heel of my palm and hoping they stay in place.

"Do you still—"

My eyes snap to Max at his soft-spoken words, silencing him instantly with whatever is on my face.

"No."

He studies me like he's sensing a lie, but for once, I am being honest. I might fight the urge every day, but I've beaten it for over a year now and I really don't want to be doubted on it.

"I'll show you if you don't believe me," I say, hooking a finger in the sleeve to tug it up, expose my forearm.

Max puts a hand on my wrist, stopping me. "I believe you."

Something inside me cracks open at those words, releasing this buildup of emotion I've kept crammed so far down I don't even recognize what it is as it swells through me.

Agony? Regret?

Relief?

Whatever it is, it saps the strength from my knees, forces me to sit on the edge of my bed so I don't collapse with it.

Max sits down beside me, a hand in my hair, scratching my scalp, until Celeste and Tasha knock on the door.

Max and I never stayed the night at each other's houses.

Mine was big enough to have Seth's friends over every weekend, but too small for one more. Pretty sure Mom and Dad thought we'd burn the house down or sneak out in the night or something.

Mr. Palazzola would've gone ballistic at the mere sight of me. Probably put down wards to keep me from stepping foot in his house like some kind of demon.

Now I have Max and two others crammed on my bed with me, with my laptop on a chair in front of us playing a horror movie that Max can't help but analyze forensically, bags of chips and candy shared between us and empty pop cans stacked on my desk.

It almost makes me sad, having them all here. It's that same nostalgic, regretful feeling I'd get every time a memory of Max would break through in the past couple years. Like I can't keep myself fully in this moment because I'm too busy dreading its end.

I don't think I ever appreciated the quiet moments like this enough when I had them before. Always too busy thinking ahead to the next adrenaline rush, or too detached to care.

Now, I don't even want to talk about myself or my wild stories. I don't need their attention when I'm perfectly content to listen to Celeste talk about how her little brothers insist their basement houses a portal to the fae realm. How she used some of her cosplay elf ears to convince them she was a faerie princess, got them to do her chores for months before their parents caught on and put an end to it.

How Tasha once took a photo in their room at night after hearing something shuffling around in the dark. How it came out distorted and washed-out, with a shadowy figure leaning in from the side, and that's when they started believing in the supernatural.

Max startles at a jump scare mid-criticizing the accuracy of a blood spatter, and when I expect Celeste to give him shit for it, she instead genuinely asks him if he wants to watch something else. Waits for him to laugh it off before making her jokes.

Tasha sits through the truly horrifying moments unblinking but gets worked up when the characters who are supposed to be friends refuse to cooperate and only make everything worse for themselves.

These are the moments when you really get to know a person.

Celeste puts up this snarky and inconsiderate front, but she watches closely. She cares.

Tasha loves people so much. Loves the human connection.

I feel out of place between them. Max is the only person I've ever cared about as much as these two seem to care about anyone and everyone, and I still never treated him as good as they're treating me only weeks after meeting.

I always put myself and my whims first.

I want to be better.

I want to be as observant as Celeste. As loving as Tasha. As selfless as Max.

But I'm just me. I can put on as convincing an act as possible, but I will still always be that.

Just me.

CHAPTER 17

I THINK MY ROOMMATE got in a fight with his girlfriend at the dance, because he actually comes back to the room that night.

He storms in, does a double take when he notices the four of us lined up against the wall, sitting on my bed. He doesn't say anything, but I can see the question in the way his face screws up.

Since when do you have friends?

It's a fair question.

We watch the last few minutes of the movie in silence, my roommate hunched at his desk and radiating anger, me dancing a coin back and forth across my knuckles to calm my nerves, and when the three of them leave, they give me sympathetic looks on their way out.

His presence on top of all the weird emotions of the night make it hard to sleep, harder to focus on finishing up this speech outline in the morning, and when Tasha messages me asking for an impromptu photoshoot, I eagerly agree just for a reason to leave the room. I send the outline off to Professor Huang just so I don't have to look at it anymore. It's not an important grade—that comes down to the speech itself.

Tasha tells me to dress casual and warm, so I throw on black jeans with only one chain, a black collared shirt under my winter flannel and my slouchy red beanie. My roommate eyeballs me on my way out, but neither of us says a word.

Tasha's waiting for me outside the dining hall with the strap of their camera bag crisscrossing their chest, an over-stuffed backpack, and two blueberry muffins in hand. They offer one to me with a bright, wide-awake smile.

"Why thank you," I say with a small bend of the knees, almost like a curtsy. "Want me to take your backpack?"

"Oh! That's okay—it's not heavy. Just a blanket and some hand warmers, in case you need a break out there."

I'm a little stunned by the thoughtfulness. Even knowing this is how Tasha is, I still feel unworthy of it. I tuck my chin and peel back the wrapper on the muffin as we head outside.

It's the warmest it's been so far this year, the snow melting in rivulets toward the lake, but when the wind picks up, it cuts right through every layer of fabric straight to the bone. I tense my shoulders to brace against it.

"How'd the rest of your night go?" Tasha asks.

I crumple the wrapper in my fist and tear the bottom off the muffin, saving the top for last. "Spent the whole night soaking in my roommate's secondhand rage." I take a bite and continue with a mouthful. "He must've got in a fight with his girlfriend. That's the first time he's slept in the room all semester."

They tilt their head to the side, swallowing their own bite of muffin before responding. "He's dating Shelby, right? I hope she's okay. She's real sweet."

"Uhh . . ." I actually have to pause and think. I've never met his girlfriend. Just assumed he has one because where else would he be staying every night?

Actually . . . do I even know his name? We never really introduced ourselves. He walked into our room for the first time on move-in day while I was in the middle of being lectured by my parents, and he just stood there in the doorway with his mom, watching my parents give me a rundown of everything they expect from me this year and all that's on the line if I fuck it up.

Great first impression.

I waited until Dad said, "Do I make myself clear?" before putting on a big smile and waving at the new arrivals over his shoulder, getting pure satisfaction out of the way Mom's and Dad's faces paled.

They were extra polite and conversational with roommate's mom then, to make up for the awkward entry, while roommate himself looked at me like he was wishing for either one of us to drop dead in that moment.

Almost a whole school year in and we haven't called each other by name, but I do remember seeing it on our door in the first week or so, before he took it down. Scottie or something like that.

"Not sure," I say finally. "I hope they make up soon, though. I like having a single." I nibble on the edge of the muffin top as Tasha leads us toward the hill up to the athletic fields.

"I'm sure Celeste already knows all the details and can keep you updated," they say.

I pull a face at them. "Okay, are we sure Celeste doesn't just use her therapist aspirations as an excuse to be nosey?"

Tasha laughs, covering their mouth with the back of their hand as they chew, puffs of frozen air misting out through their gloved fingers. They're wearing an oversized black sweater that hangs to their knees and covers their hands almost entirely, a heavy winter coat on over that and boots meant for the snow, ready to be outside for a while.

"She is quite nosey," Tasha agrees, smiling when they lower their hand again. "But it's because she worries. About everyone. She wants to know everything so she can step in to help when she's needed."

The hike up the hill is enough to warm me up a bit, get Tasha to lose the coat (I carry it for them), and as we continue past the fields and onto the path through the snowed-over golf course, I picture myself sitting on a couch across from Celeste, her with a notepad, jotting down my inner-most thoughts.

Where would I even begin?

I don't know who I am as a person, but whoever it is, I don't think I like him very much.

Or maybe, *Sometimes I don't feel real and, honestly, I think I prefer it that way.*

Tasha slips their hand into mine and gives it a soft squeeze, startling me back into my body just as I start to float out of my head. I look down at the point of contact between us.

A hand to hold. A friend to keep me grounded.

"What about you?" they ask.

I shift my eyes to their face to find them looking straight ahead. "Huh?"

They squeeze my hand again. "I want to be a photographer. Celeste wants to be a therapist. Max is studying forensics. What about you?"

"Oh." I dodge around a slush puddle in the path, plowed to allow access to the trails in the woods. "I don't really know yet. My mom says I should go into coaching, but I, uh, lack the leadership qualities, to say the least."

Tasha shakes their head. "I think when it comes to things like that, you develop them over time. As long as you have the knowledge and the passion, you can make it work."

I shrug one shoulder dismissively. "I don't know—I guess

I just can't see myself doing it, and even if I did, that's not a stable career unless you're coaching in a pro league. I'm not delusional enough to aspire to that."

"Hmm, well, what about when you were a kid? What did you dream about being when you grew up?"

I open my mouth to answer, expecting it to fall right off my tongue. It should be easy. Like . . . a firefighter, or an actor, teacher, doctor, all those common dream jobs kids seem to cycle through. But as I think back, trying to remember anything about my childhood, everything starts to close in around me like my brain is putting blinders on me.

I don't remember anything. Nothing substantial at least, outside of, well. The bad things.

"I . . ."

Come on. Nothing? Just make something up, or commiserate on how ridiculous it is to send your kid to an expensive-ass private college when they don't even know what they want to do with their life, don't just—

"That's okay," Tasha cuts in. "You have time. We're not even allowed to declare majors till next year."

I sigh, grateful for the out. "Yeah."

"You like the woods?" They look up at me with these big, hopeful eyes, and I kind of feel like even if I hated the woods, I'd still say yes just for them.

"Totally. Makes me feel like Aragorn. Or maybe more like Jaskier."

Tasha snorts. "You're definitely more of a Jaskier."

I nudge them with my elbow, grinning. "Why do you say that like it's a bad thing?"

"I didn't!"

We step into the woods off the edge of the golf course, discussing the merits of strong, woodsy ranger types versus pretty boy bards. We're both in agreement that the pretty boys always come out on top.

"So the theme of this photoshoot is pretty boy in the woods then?" I say as they pose me on a log half-submerged in the sluggish creek cutting through the trees.

They take a quick candid shot, and smile. "I need you to embody your inner Aragorn and Jaskier all at once."

I'm way too scrawny to pull off either of them, but I make sure to give them my absolute best. Hiding my face in the shadows of my hood to brood like Strider for one shot, dip my chin and make eyes at the camera for the next, knowing Tasha's talent will make something out of it all.

At first, I'm just trying to look good. Arranging my face and my body in those enticing ways I've seen in viral thirst traps. Really embrace my obnoxious e-boy aesthetic and put out the cocky, sexual energy people expect from me.

And Tasha seems happy with it. Smiles when I shift into a new pose. Laughs at my borderline flirtatious comments. Even gets flustered a few times.

But after a while, it just feels so fake. So ridiculous.

Like, who do I think I am? Going from an identity crisis ten minutes ago to thinking I'm some kind of model?

If anyone who knew me in high school could see me right now, they'd laugh in my face.

I let the act fall away bit by bit, my face dropping into something more neutral, maybe even a little downcast, shoulders slouching, hands tucked away into my sleeves. I hop down off the log and walk along the soggy bank, kicking through stubborn snow drifts and snapping frozen twigs underfoot.

Tasha trails behind me, then steps off to the side, then jogs ahead to walk backward in front of me, still snapping pictures. They're not smiling or laughing anymore. They have this serious, focused look on their face like this is what they wanted to begin with.

So I walk. I don't pose. I don't put on a show. I just exist and let Tasha do what they're best at.

And maybe . . . maybe I should try being real with them for once.

"Hey, so . . ." I slide my hands into my pockets, look off to the left, across the creek, into the depths of the woods.

Tasha takes the shot, then lowers their camera slightly to look at me with their own eyes. "What's up?"

"Celeste said something to me last night, after you ran inside for the water."

Their eyes go wide and distant, like they're running through every embarrassing thing they've ever revealed to Celeste.

"Nothing bad," I add before they can spiral too far into panic, but they still look at me apprehensively. "She just said you care about me a lot, or something."

Their whole body instantly relaxes, and they roll their eyes, releasing a small huff. "Well, yeah. Of course I do."

But I don't relax. I stop with my shoes sinking into the slush and decomposed leaves, squeezing moisture out of the muffin wrapper in my pocket as I press my fingernails into my palm, the other clenched around my deck of cards.

"But why?"

I don't realize how pathetic a question that is until I watch their face crumple, their eyes shimmer.

"Because you're a person, Nathaniel," they say, so very earnest. "And you're my friend."

I shake my head, the static buzz of anxiety building in my chest and stealing away my breath.

Why am I trying to sabotage this? Just accept their friendship and shut the fuck up.

"We just met," I say. "You don't even know me."

"I'm trying to." They take a single step forward, holding a hand out like an offer. "I am. I know what it's like, pretending to be something you're not. I did that my whole life before I realized I'm nonbinary. It's different, yeah, but I know you do it too. You pretend to be a worse person than you are."

I scoff. Take one hand out of my pocket to scrub at the side of my face. "I literally brag about my criminal record, Tasha."

They take another step forward, hand still out. "Exactly."

The trees have blocked most of that biting wind while we've been out here, but I feel it now. Standing in front of Tasha with them looking at me like I matter, like I mean something to them, I feel cold right down to the core. I should drop it. Accept their faith in me and use it as motivation to meet their expectations. Strive to be worthy of their care.

But I can't. I can't accept something I don't deserve.

I shake my head again, stepping back. "I'm not pretending. If anything, I'm worse than you think."

"I don't believe that for a second. I've seen the different ways you act, how you'll get quiet and self-conscious and then force yourself to be loud and cocky. It's not hard to notice, Nathaniel. After we left you that night when you jumped out the window? One conversation with you and Celeste and I knew we needed to help you."

"Oh."

If I thought I was cold before, well, now it feels like I've taken a plunge into the creek.

"That's why you guys wanted me around so much," I say.

"I wondered why I was making friends so easily. That's never happened to me before."

Tasha closes their eyes and presses their hand to their forehead, sighing deeply. "No, that's not . . . I know how that sounded, but I'm hanging out with you because I like you, okay? And so does Celeste. And we look after our friends."

"I don't need anyone to look after me, Tasha. I've managed this long on my own."

"Have you?" Their voice cracks. I can see the wobble of their chin as they struggle to hold back their emotion. Their camera hangs from the strap around their neck. The burble of water and the creaking of the trees on the wind are the only sounds between us.

We stare at each other for a few long moments, them with desperation in their eyes and me entirely empty before I say, definitively, "Yes," and turn around, heading back the way we came. I get a few feet of distance before I hear them follow.

It's the truth. There's a difference between managing and thriving. I've survived to this point, so yeah, I'm managing.

As for thriving, well.

It doesn't matter how many chances people give me, how many opportunities to move forward and get better they lay out in front of me.

I will always ruin it for myself.

CHAPTER 18

I DON'T GO TO the lacrosse games on Sunday, and when Max meets me for breakfast Monday morning, he doesn't ask.

Next time I see Celeste is Tuesday, when she slaps her hand down on the table where I'm scribbling spirals in my public speaking notebook, making me flinch. I rein it in before looking up at her. She stands on the other side of the table, leaning forward so she can loom over me with her fist on her hip.

"You made Tasha cry."

I blink at her slowly, holding eye contact. "I didn't do anything."

"You were a *dick*."

I sit back in my chair with a shrug, pulling my notebook along with me to keep doodling. "Yeah, well."

"Yeah, well, nothing. The act was fun and interesting at first, but if you're actually going to start hurting Tasha's feelings, it can stop right the fuck now."

"Who ever said it was an act?"

Mickey sits gingerly in his chair at the other end of the table, like he's trying so hard not to make a sound and draw attention to himself. I turn my head to look at him and he winces.

"It's obvious," Celeste seethes. "Which is the only reason it was interesting to begin with."

She's not talking loudly, but it's a small classroom, and everyone's eyes are on us as they settle into their seats.

I should be embarrassed, getting reamed out like this in front of the whole class. Just like I should've been embarrassed when I became a meme for jumping out that window, or every time someone refers to me as obnoxious.

But I don't have the energy for embarrassment.

"I'm not trying to be interesting," I say blandly. "But everyone always seems so interested anyway."

Celeste's lip curls in disgust. She looks at me like she's really seeing me for the first time, and she hates whatever she's found.

That's okay. With how much I hate myself, it only makes sense for everyone else to hate me too.

I look back at her with complete apathy, and before anything else can be said, Professor Huang comes in and starts setting up for class. Celeste reluctantly takes her seat next to me. She's either too stubborn to give up the seat she's had all semester because of me, or it's not as serious as she's making it out to be and she'll be over it by the end of class.

It's not like I went and insulted Tasha or anything, after all. I was honest, the way they both asked me to be. The way they haven't been with me, apparently.

Professor Huang finishes arranging her papers and then glances up at the class.

No, she glances up at *me*. I watch as she chews the inside of her cheek, adjusts her glasses, and then pads over to me. She leans in close and speaks low enough to avoid too many people overhearing, and says, "See me after class, Mr. Conti." She taps once on the table beside my elbow and returns to her seat at the front of the room to get class started.

The hour is passed discussing how and when to inject humor into speeches, especially with serious subjects, but I have nothing to contribute. Why would she need to talk to me after class?

My outline couldn't have been so bad she needs to go over it with me like that. I had an A– in this class last I checked. I'm a decent writer and an entertaining speaker—she's told me herself. There shouldn't be an issue.

Professor Huang has barely opened her mouth to dismiss class before Celeste is up and out of the room. Mickey sighs heavily, watching her go.

"I've never seen her like that before," he says.

"Don't you barely even know each other?"

I keep my eyes forward, but I can picture that ever-present blankness on his face as he stares me down, closing his notebook and tucking it under his arm. He shuffles his feet, takes a breath like he's going to say something.

Maybe he does. I don't really know. The sound of my own breathing drowns out everything else, swirling behind my eardrums on the way down as I watch Professor Huang pack away her things. I feel Mickey leave more than I see or hear it, and when Professor Huang looks at me, I stand, slinging my bag over my shoulder and slipping my hands in my pockets as I approach her table.

She looks up at me from behind rose gold, circle-framed glasses, the bangs of her graying black hair falling into her eyes. She lets me brew in the suspense for a moment before reaching into the bag at her feet and setting a thick stack of papers on the table between us. The cover page is blank except for my name in the center.

"What happened, Nathaniel?" she asks, folding her hands in front of her.

I glance between her face and the paper. "What do you mean?"

Professor Huang starts slowly flipping through the pages as she speaks. "I was very excited to read this one. I knew this assignment would be better suited to your storytelling style. I was a little worried about the length, for a ten-minute speech, but I still had high hopes. But . . ."

The pages start out looking like a normal outline. Section headings and bulleted points as a guide, longer blocks of text where I wanted to make sure I got my wording down right. But after a few pages, things start getting a little . . . messy. Pages and pages of empty space. Like I was leaning in on the *enter* key. One full page without a bullet point or paragraph break. Some wild font changes.

"Most of what is written here is incomprehensible," she says. I can't judge her tone of voice. She's got that professor cadence, rich and soothing and all-knowing, but I can't tell if that's a tinge of concern or irritation I'm hearing.

I'd rather her be mad at me than worried for me.

But then she adds, "And what is written is . . . well, it's concerning, Nathaniel."

Fuck.

She didn't even bother to mark up any pages after the first two, and there's no grade circled at the end like usual. I thumb through the pages, skimming some of what's written, and I don't remember any of this beyond the first couple of pages. The pages I worked on Saturday morning before going out with Tasha.

"I didn't write this, Professor Huang," I say, dead serious. "I mean, I wrote *this*." I motion to the normal section, then flip to where things go wrong. "But not this."

She raises an eyebrow.

"Really, I don't know what happened. My roommate doesn't like me—maybe he got into my laptop and messed with it?"

"That's a lot of effort to go through to mess with your roommate," she says.

"I–I don't know what happened, I don't—"

She puts her hands on the table and pushes herself to her feet. I stagger back a step as she comes around the table, my hands twisted in my shirt and my breath coming quick and shallow like my chest is too small for my lungs.

"Hey." Professor Huang reaches a hand out but doesn't touch me. "It's all right. The outlines aren't worth much. Recover what you can and give as good a speech as I know you're capable of, and I'll drop this one, all right?"

I clench my jaw and nod once, breathe through my nose, slow and shaky. Professor Huang looks at me way too closely.

Get it together. Don't fall apart with an audience.

Come on.

I clench my messed-up assignment in both hands and rush out of the room. I read the whole thing as I make my way across campus. Professor Huang was right. It is concerning.

Concerning in a way that makes my forearms itch. Concerning in a way that's actually triggering. Makes me think I probably definitely shouldn't be alone right now.

Concerning in a way that means I did write this, even if it wasn't consciously.

It rambles about things I have never admitted to anyone. Not even Max. Not even to myself. Goes into detail about things I refuse to think about, and when I do anyway, it means I'm in a dangerous position.

I thought I was doing better. Mostly better. Sure, there's moments where my mind slips. Moments that seem utterly bleak. Even some extended periods of misery and hopelessness here and there.

But if I can sit down and write pages and pages recounting these things and turn it in to my professor without even thinking about it or remembering it, then something is very, very wrong.

My hands are shaking by the time I reach the door to my building. I shouldn't be alone right now. My roommate, Scottie or whatever the fuck his name is, might be in the room, but if he's not, the solitude might be too much, and if he is, well, I'm not sure even that'll help in the long run.

I crush the paper between my hands and tilt my head back, sighing at the gray winter sky. Celeste is mad at me and Tasha is upset, and they were never really my friends to begin with.

There's only one option.

I take out my phone, and I text Max.

CHAPTER 19

MAX HAS SOME CHEMISTRY midterm exam prep he can't skip.

He tells me to sit in the dining hall and wait for him, but the buzz of anxiety makes my stomach uneasy and being surrounded by the smell of food and the sounds of people eating makes me nauseous before long. So I head across campus to the library instead.

It's quieter than the dining hall, less crowded, more dangerous, but less likely to make me sick. I walk around for a bit before I make my way to that wide-open area on the second floor where a few study carrels are taken, people with their heads bent over laptops or textbooks, earbuds in.

No one so much as glances in my direction as I throw myself into a seat at one of the open tables, but at least I'm not alone.

I don't know how long I sit there for. Staring off at the wall of windows overlooking campus and the lake, not really seeing it. Long enough for a couple other students to pack up their things and leave. I only notice because one of them walks too close and their bag brushes against my shoulder, snapping me out of my head.

Not long enough for Max to be out of his class.

I take out my phone to check on the time, and it's been maybe ten minutes. Ten minutes that felt like ten hours that felt like ten seconds.

With my phone out, I go to my email, pull up the message I sent to Professor Huang to see it for myself.

Hey Professor Huang, just wanted to send this in early for your opinion so I can get this speech down good. Thanks, Nathaniel

I click open the attachment, see the same title page with just my name, scroll down through the pages I remember cleaning up on Saturday morning. I didn't think to check the page count, scroll down past the actual outline, past blank pages, to see what I'd done during those days after Max showed up, when I dissociated for a week.

I stand up and pace for a couple minutes before I start getting dirty looks, and that only makes me feel worse, so I sit back down. Take out a notebook and a pen. Think about how I can possibly salvage this outline without spiraling out of control.

Talk about a defining moment in your life. If you could pinpoint a single moment or event that made you who you are today, what would it be?

A bullet point in the syllabus says *This assignment has the potential to get deeply personal. Please put your own mental health and safety first when deciding your topic.*

I started out writing about that police chase, because it was my first interaction with law enforcement without Max there to back me up. The first time I did something so reckless after that armed robbery charge. It's what got me kicked off the lacrosse team and revealed my unhealthy coping mechanisms and—

Maybe that's why my thought process devolved so entirely when trying to write about it.

I don't like to acknowledge what I used to do to myself because it only makes me want to do it again. Forcing myself to write down those words, what the doctors saw when they went to set my broken wrist . . . It must have triggered that spiral. The mess that this outline became.

The pen clatters onto the table when I press the heels of my hands into my eyes.

Professor Huang warned us not to push ourselves deeper than we're comfortable with. Told us our safety comes first. Maybe that's why I went with this, instead of the actual thing that made me into the utter shitbag of a human I am today.

Because if writing about the second worst time of my life was enough to decimate me like this, I might never recover from writing about the first.

Maybe I won't even recover from thinking about it.

Now that it's crossed my mind, that's where it sticks.

It wasn't even the actual *thing* that fucked me up the most. At least I don't think it was. Not really.

It's the way it was handled by my family.

The way it was handled by me.

Because when my cousin Gianna came forward about what happened to her, the whole family turned on her. Well, first they went to all the girl cousins and asked if the same thing had happened to them, and when all of them said no, that's when they tore her apart, along with Aunt Rosa. Said they were just trying to ruin our uncle's life, and since he was the baby of the family, all the aunts and uncles came together to support him and shun Gianna and Rosa.

And I just sat and watched it all happen. Never once spoke up in Gianna's defense. Let everyone call her a liar, even though I knew.

I knew she was telling the truth.

Because it happened to me too.

But I was a boy, and no one thought to ask me.

I don't think I've ever looked at any of my cousins the same after that.

I look at the girls and wonder if they lied when their parents asked them, because they were embarrassed or afraid.

I look at the boys and wonder if they had to bite their tongue and look away in shame while the adults burned Gianna at the stake.

I wouldn't blame them if they did. I couldn't. Because I did the same thing.

But I can blame myself.

If I had spoken up, even if no one believed me, at least Gianna wouldn't have been alone. At least she'd know someone other than her mother believed her.

Maybe I would've been shunned by the family too, called attention-seeking and a liar.

But they call me those things now anyway, and if I'd said something then, at least I wouldn't have to deal with this crushing guilt.

I would rather be mind-numbingly sad at all times than deal with the guilt. Knowing I could've made a difference, helped my cousin, and instead chose to watch her suffer.

Because I was too afraid.

Too ashamed.

I think that was the moment I well and truly started to hate myself.

SETH ANSWERS THE PHONE when I call.

It catches me so off guard that I don't respond until he adds, "Nathaniel? You there?"

"Yeah." I'm in one of the library's bathrooms, alone but still almost whispering. The way that single word echoes, I bet everyone in the building can hear me.

"What's up?" Seth asks.

"You remember G?" I blurt out.

I can practically hear him blinking in surprise. "Uh, you mean our cousin? Of course."

"Why did no one believe her?"

Seth is rational and reasonable and he knows everything. He must have this figured out.

He inhales sharply through his teeth. "Wow. Not the conversation I was expecting to have today." There's some shuffling in the background, distant voices, then silence. For a second I think he's hung up on me, until he says, "I don't think it had anything to do with G. You remember how they all talked about Auntie Rosa?"

"Not really." We're only a year apart, Seth and me. That he remembers things like that and I don't probably has something to do with, I don't know, trauma.

"They always ostracized her, talked behind her back about her being too feminist, too liberal, not godly enough. From what I gathered, all the siblings assumed G said something innocuous and Rosa blew it out of proportion."

I turn the sink on and off as he speaks, chew the inside of my mouth to shreds like it'll help distance me from his words.

"Is that what you think?" I ask.

"Me? I don't know, Nathaniel, we were kids. I didn't even realize what was going on till I got older and thought back on it." A door opens in the background and someone calls out to Seth. His voice is muffled when he responds, then says to me, "Hey, I gotta go, but . . . are you all right?"

"Huh?" I turn the sink off. "Yeah. Obviously."

"This was just—"

"Research," I say. "For a sociology assignment. Thanks for the help."

I hang up before he can answer.

CHAPTER 20

I TRY TO REDO this outline. I really do.

I put in earbuds and turn on some relaxing thunderstorm ambience to drown out my thoughts of everything Seth said and put pen to paper, but I don't write a word.

I don't want to be defined by my guilt, or the shitty things that have happened to me. I don't want to be defined by how much I hate myself.

Maybe I don't even want to be *the obnoxious e-boy*, or the guy who crashes parties and jumps out of windows.

Maybe I just want to be Nathaniel. Whatever the fuck that means.

Nathaniel, the guy who . . .

I press the pen into the paper, hard. Try again.

Nathaniel Conti, who . . .

I can't think of a single positive thing.

I am not anything.

I am nothing.

I'm . . .

Fuck.

Who the fuck am I?

I take out my cards. Try to focus on flourishes to recenter my mind. But my hands are so unsteady, I end up spraying the entire deck across the table.

I stand so suddenly my chair almost topples. Push my fingers into my hair. Turn in a circle. Grit my teeth to keep from screaming because I don't know if I'd ever be able to stop.

My heart feels like it's trying to crack through my sternum. Like even my own organs hate me enough that they want out.

Like fuck, man, I don't want to be here either, but I can't really do anything about it, can I?

Okay, maybe if I look at it this way. Not who the fuck am I, but who the fuck do I want to be? What's that thing we learned in sociology? Dramaturgy. Maybe I need to throw the whole self-presentation bullshit out the window, stop putting on a show for others and live for myself.

I just don't know what that *means*.

I don't know what that means and I don't know how to figure it out when all I can think about is the nasty things my mother and my aunts and uncles said about Gianna and how I could have stopped it but I didn't and now she has to live her life with not only the trauma of what was done to her, but also the trauma of her whole extended family making her the villain and her abuser the victim.

I hate myself.

I hate myself and I want to—my nails catch on a ridge of scar tissue and I wince, looking down to see my right hand shoved into my left sleeve, scratching. I yank my hand away and clench it into a tight fist.

This is bad.

My breathing is too thin and rattly and I don't feel strong enough or stable enough to resist this. I don't want to relapse, dammit, I don't.

There's an abandoned backpack hanging on the back of the chair at one of the study carrels.

It's a shitty fucking coping mechanism, sure, but at least it's better than carving myself open.

I give a cursory glance around the area and everyone either has their back turned or their head down and the walls of the carrel hide what I'm doing as I slip my hand in the bag. It must be one of the carrels rented out by semester, a dedicated study space for only one student. It's got photos taped up on the walls: a roster shot of the Hartland Royals men's hockey team, but they're all laughing and draped over each other like it's an outtake. Two white guys in graduation robes and costume sunglasses and plastic crowns, holding senior mugs with their arms slung over each other's shoulders. A Boston Bruins logo. More Royals hockey players. Even Mickey. Art of some fantasy characters.

I feel a frown taking hold as I root around in this guy's

backpack, feeling the edges of books, the spirals of a note-book, the cold plastic of a laptop. A few loose pens. Even taking things right out of people's pockets feels less personal than this sneak peek into his life.

My fingers brush the leather of a wallet, and I tug it out quickly. It's white, covered in dice and cartoon weapons and roses. I flip it open and check the ID first. Luca Cicero, with this big goofy grin and dark hair flopping into his eyes. He has no cash or credit cards. Just a debit card from a Boston community bank and a coupon for the Throne Room.

I'm about to pocket both when I feel the presence of someone looming behind me. I bite my tongue and close the wallet with a *snap*, dropping it back into the bag and turning around with excuses primed and ready.

Max.

It's just Max.

That might actually be worse than if it were a campus safety officer, or Luca Cicero himself.

His arms are crossed all sternly, but his face is passive. There's no judgment or disappointment there, even if there should be. Even though I kind of want to see it. *Need* to see it.

"Honor Code, Nat," he says when I offer no explanation. His voice is flat. "You'll get kicked out."

I push my tongue between my lips as I consider what to say. They're so dry, I feel them peeling.

"Maybe I want to get kicked out."

"Then *drop* out," he argues. "Don't ruin your chances of transferring somewhere else."

I push past him, away from Luca Cicero's backpack before he can catch us hovering over his things.

"It's like you said," I say as he follows. "I was always so anti-college, right? What the fuck am I even doing here? Why would I want to go anywhere else?"

He matches my frenzied pace as I march toward the stairs, down to the first floor, out the door, and into the cold air of the tail end of winter in Central New York. But when the door swings shut behind us and I'm still moving, he reaches out and snatches my wrist in his hand, tugging me to a standstill.

He can't feel what's under his hand, under the layers of sleeves, but he *knows*, and even that is too much.

"What happened?" he asks.

My breath catches in my throat, and when it breaks through, it shudders in and gasps out and then I think I must be sobbing, because my hands are pressed to my eyes and I can't breathe at all.

Max's hands clasp hard onto my shoulders. My feet move with him as he pushes me back, until he's holding me against the outside wall of the library, the brick digging into my back.

I snap out of it so suddenly, I'm sure it gives Max whiplash. I clamp my mouth shut to stifle one last gasping breath and lower my hands, schooling my face into the same indifference Max always wears. I press my fingers to the sharp edges of brick behind me and look out over his shoulder at the lake down the hill.

We're under the library's overhang, with its small patio half-enclosed by the same kind of naked shrubs that scratched me up weeks ago. It's quiet. Private. No one around to witness this breakdown.

But I'm not about to unload my problems onto Max. Not when he's just come back into my life and he's doing so well. I can't drag him back down with me.

He blinks at me, and when he asks again, "What happened?," there's desperation in his voice.

"Nothing," I say. "I'm all right."

He drops his hands off my shoulders just to push them into his hair, let them sit on top of his head as he heaves out a breath, cheeks puffing with it. "Yeah, real convincing, Nat."

I shrug, and Max doesn't say anything else. He watches me closely, while I stare blankly back at him.

This is better. Maybe this is what I should strive for. Emptiness. If I hollow myself out, remove all feeling, there won't be anything left to self-destruct over.

Or maybe I should walk out into the lake. Right along the bottom, out into the middle. Cayuga isn't the largest of the Finger Lakes, but it is the widest, especially here by campus. I'd get exhausted long before I made it back to shore.

I think I want to die.

"*Nat.*"

That desperate pitch in Max's voice is even more pronounced now. I finally meet his eyes. "What?"

"Don't–you . . . you really want to die?"

"What?" Did I say that out loud? I shake my head. "No."

"You just *said so.*"

Well, shit.

"No I didn't."

He sets his jaw, and for once he doesn't look apathetic or smug. He looks scared, his bottom lip trembling and his eyes misting over. He turns his back on me, and for a second I'm sure I'm losing him again, just like I did before.

He takes a moment to breathe, and just when I think he's going to walk away, he faces me again and steps closer instead, leaning against the wall beside me. He jams his hands into his pockets, his arm cocked out so his elbow presses into my arm.

"Do you remember the time I asked you why you like to steal and vandalize and cause trouble?" he asks. "When we filled a whole backpack with shit from the bulk aisle at Tops and snuck into the drive-in to see the new *Conjuring* movie?"

I shake my head. We did a lot of snack stealing and drive-in sneaking, but I don't remember him ever asking me that, or what I would've said.

"You told me you were bored and it was fun. And you

looked at me like I was an idiot for even asking. But I know it's not true."

I push off the wall and start walking. I need to move. If I keep standing here, with my back to the wall, listening to whatever Max is getting at, I might start to disintegrate.

He falls into step beside me, and he keeps talking. "It was never about the fun, or the thrill, or any of the excuses you make."

"Then what's it about, Max?" I want to snap it at him, but I don't have the energy. The words tumble out listlessly. "Tell me. Why do I steal and vandalize and cause trouble?"

He takes a long step to get in front of me, forcing me to stop.

"You want to get caught." He says it so matter-of-factly, like he's so damn sure of himself. Like he knows me so freaking well, when I don't even know myself. "You want to get caught because that's the only time your mom and dad pay any attention to you. You want to get caught because you want someone to realize what's going on and step in to help you."

This should hurt. My best friend in my face reminding me that my parents don't give a shit.

But it's nothing new, and it doesn't hurt me anymore.

I shrug. Avoid eye contact. "There's nothing going on, and I don't need help."

"Bullshit."

"I don't know what you want from me."

"I want some honesty from you, Nat."

I laugh. I don't mean to. It just happens, this completely unhinged burst of giggles. I press the back of my hand against my mouth to stifle it and turn my head so I don't have to look at him anymore.

"You should know by now," I say. "Nothing about me is honest."

When I step around him again, I don't expect him to follow. It was an obvious *conversation over* thing to say, but he doesn't let me get half a step before he's right at my elbow, giving me no space to breathe.

He returns my dumbfounded look with a click of his tongue. "You just told me you want to die. I'm not leaving you alone."

I sigh heavily. Try to rub away the headache building behind my eyebrows.

And when I laugh again, it's not crazed or derisive. It's all relief, and maybe a little bit of gratitude.

CHAPTER 21

IT'S NOT THAT I actually want to die.

Not really.

It's more that I don't want to exist anymore.

There's a difference.

Max stays with me the rest of the day. He sits in my room and makes small talk with Scottie when he's around, while I lie flat on my back, staring up at the ceiling, fanning out a fresh deck of cards with one hand, collapsing them back together, fanning them out again. The weight of him on the edge of my mattress and the low rumble of his voice as he laughs with Scottie keep me tethered.

I can't decide if I appreciate it or not.

I don't really want to be in my body right now. I especially don't want to be in my head. But his presence forces me to stay.

At dinnertime, instead of dragging me down to the dining hall, he calls up the Throne Room and orders us chicken fingers and loaded fries and pays extra to have it delivered to my room so I don't have to leave and he doesn't have to leave me.

He even stays the night. Sleeps on the floor beside my bed, covered by the throw blanket Scottie had stuffed into his closet after the fight with his girlfriend. I think he appreciates having Max here more than I do. Someone he can actually talk to that doesn't weird him out, makes the room less awkward.

This is just like Max. Give up his whole day and night just to sit around and keep an eye on me while I have a crisis, even making a friend in the process.

He's always put me ahead of himself. Maybe if he thought of his own well-being every once in a while, he wouldn't have a criminal record to deal with.

In the morning, when Scottie's gone and Max and I are about to head out to his room so he can get dressed in his own clean clothes, I speak for the first time since we left the library.

"If you were always so sure I wanted to get caught, why did you go along with it?"

Max shakes his head. I expect a smile and a brush-off, something like, *Couldn't let you have all the fun.* What I get instead is a dead-serious look and a stern, "If I couldn't talk you out of it, I might as well be there to keep you safe while you did it."

He zips his jacket all the way up and tucks his chin into the collar, hands in the pockets like that's that.

"You could've talked me out of it," I say.

It must be too quiet to hear. He pulls his mouth out of the collar again, eyebrows furrowed, and goes, "Huh?"

"You could've talked me out of it, Max. I would've listened to anything you said."

He does smile this time, but it's one of those thin-lipped ones, the corners of his mouth pulled back instead of up. It looks kind of sad. "Well then, I'm sorry I never tried."

"No, that's—I'm not trying to make you feel bad. I'm just saying."

I can't tell what he's thinking. Max has never been easy to read, with that constant stoicism he holds on to, but the years between us have made it impossible. Maybe he doesn't believe me at all, and he's just continuing to go along with whatever I say.

Max might have taken the fall for a lot of the things I've done, but I never thought of him as a pushover. Was I really walking all over him for our entire friendship?

"Something to keep in mind going forward," he says. "I'm gonna be late if we don't get going. C'mon."

And there's the brush-off. He steps past me toward the door, and all I can do is follow, chin tucked to my chest and eyes locked on my feet.

Have I mentioned how much I *hate* the feeling of guilt? I want to shove a hand under my rib cage and root around until I find the rotting source of it in my chest cavity, scrape it out with my fingernails before it can spread uncontrollably through my whole being.

I don't want to be that toxic friend that all of Max's other friends rally against to convince him to cut out.

I don't want to be a source of trauma for him, any more than I already have been.

If I won't be better for myself or my parents, I can at least be better for him.

"You gonna be okay today?" he asks as we get to the point where we go our separate ways. Him to his room to get ready for class, me . . .

Wherever.

I nod, hands stuffed in my pockets, unable to make eye contact. "I don't actually want to die, you know. Just an intrusive thought that made its way out."

He gives me that look that means he can see right through me.

"I'll skip class," he says.

"No! I'll be fine. Don't tank your grades for me."

He keeps looking at me for another moment or two, chewing the inside of his cheek as he considers what to do. I try not to squirm or look away, appear as mentally stable as possible.

Finally, he scrubs a hand over his face with a heavy sigh. "Okay, but if I text you and you don't respond, I'm sending Celeste after you. Got it?"

My first instinct is to argue. To insist I'm fine, that he doesn't have to worry about me or check up on me or even care about me at all.

"Okay," I say instead. "Thank you."

Because he deserves a little gratitude.

"I'll stop by after classes," he says. He brushes a light touch against my elbow and jogs up the steps to the front door of his building.

I stand there for a minute or two after he's gone, waiting to see where my mind will go. I'm tempted to go back to my room. Get back in bed. Let the weight of the blankets hold my body down while my head escapes for a few hours.

But standing here, staring at the ridges of dirty snow along the edges of the sidewalk, melting down the hill toward the lake, I feel firmly rooted. Max put in all that effort. He insists on caring about me, so I should at least put in some effort of my own.

I take a deep breath. Let the cold air wake me up.

And I go to class.

CHAPTER 22

THERE'S A KNOCK ON my door later that day as I'm juggling my cards at my bedroom window, debating whether to go to dinner or ask Max to bring me something up.

I glance over my shoulder, avoid looking at my reflection in the mirror on the back of the door. It could be Max. Or my RA making a wellness check at his behest.

Or it could be the cops, here to bring me into the hospital because I'm a danger to myself.

Another knock startles a flinch out of me.

"Let us in, Conti. We need to talk."

Or it's Celeste, here to yell at me some more.

I take a deep breath and sigh to myself before sinking into my desk chair, bracing for impact. "Door's open."

I expect her to come in hot, launch right into a diatribe against my character, red-faced and fuming.

But she opens the door cautiously, peeks her head in all nervously before taking a step inside, trailed closely by Tasha.

There's a sharp twist in my chest at the sight of their swollen eyes, like they've been crying. I run my thumb across the edge of my deck and chew my lip, dropping my gaze to the floor at their feet.

Celeste closes the door behind them and takes a position in the middle of the room like she's approaching the stand at a trial, fists clenched at her sides. Tasha stands just behind her, shifting their weight from foot to foot.

There's only a moment of silence before Celeste inhales slowly through her nose and says, calm and serious, her tone deeper than usual like she's embodying her future as a therapist, "Tasha and I talked about what happened, and I understand why you would be upset with us after that. I'm sorry I came at you like that yesterday. All I cared about was that Tasha was upset and I blamed you without real reason. I'm sorry."

I open my mouth to brush it off, tell a joke, at least laugh. Nothing comes out. I don't have it in me to try for anything but the truth right now.

My mouth closes slowly, jaw clenching. I swallow a lump of emotion swelling in my throat and blink away the haze in my vision.

Celeste sighs softly, settling onto the edge of my bed. "Listen . . . I know I'm not very tactful, with the way I get into people's business and ask personal questions. I've mentioned my brothers before, how close we are, but. My older brother?

He dealt with depression his whole life and never said anything to anyone. He killed himself a couple years ago."

There's that twisting in my chest again.

"At the time, it seemed like it was out of nowhere," Celeste continues quickly, like she's trying to avoid condolences. "But looking back, there were signs that we overlooked. If I think about it too hard, the guilt . . . it's crushing. If only I'd paid more attention, maybe I could have helped him. I am *never* going to let that happen again."

"Something like that . . . it wasn't your fault," I say. Maybe she doesn't want condolences, but she needs to know that at least.

She shakes her head. "I know that. But that guilty feeling creeps in anyway."

I wince, look down at my lap. That's a sentiment I can relate to.

"The point is, I started talking to you because I was a little worried for you, yeah. But that's not why I wanted to hang out with you, or why I became friends with you."

"Me neither," Tasha adds, quiet and sincere.

They have no reason to lie. Unless they're afraid to push me over the edge or something.

But I can't help but think back to the careful way Celeste puts makeup on me. The way Tasha's eyes light up when I look at them. The easy way they accepted me into their lives, and then Max with me.

I could see my bond with them growing as deep as the one I have with Max. Maybe even more, without the troubled history between us.

So I nod. Lift my chin and look my friends in the eye.

"I want this to work," I say. "I really do. But I'm such a . . . such a mess, I don't know how. You'll get sick of waiting for me to figure myself out, or I'll do something to piss you off."

Tasha shakes their head, closing the distance between us to crouch down in front of me. "We're college freshmen. None of us really has ourselves completely figured out. You don't like who you are now, you don't think you're a good person? Well now you can choose to be one going forward. And if you piss us off, we'll talk about it, just like we'll talk about it if we piss you off."

Celeste scoffs, and then immediately sniffles. Tasha and I both look over in time to watch her wipe at her eyes with her knuckles. "You make it sound like we're all dating. Both of you."

A laugh bursts out of me, loosening up that painful tension around my heart. I brush my hair out of my eyes and leave my hand resting on the top of my head. I take an easy breath in and hold it as Tasha chuckles.

"Queerplatonic soulmates?" they offer.

Celeste smiles through her tears. "Honestly? I could see it going that way."

I close my eyes with a smile. These past few days—this whole semester, really—has been one instance of emotional whiplash after another.

But with Tasha and Celeste and Max by my side, I know I'll get through whatever is thrown at me next.

CHAPTER 23

TASHA WANTS ME TO dress up for their art show on Saturday. Like I'm their muse or something and they want to show me off.

Or maybe because it's a big deal for them and I'm tangentially a part of it and they don't want me to embarrass them, I don't know.

So I put on a white dress shirt and smooth down the wrinkles. It would look better if I rolled the sleeves to my elbows, but that's out of the question. The black vest over the top of it helps, along with tucking it all into a pair of black dress pants that fit me exquisitely and topping it all off with a black tie and a short silver chain on my belt. I don't have any nice, dressy shoes, so I take a wad of wet paper towels to the scuffs on my Vans and say good enough.

Gel my hair so it floats off my forehead. Dab pink and black shadows under my eyes.

I stand in front of the mirror that's on the back of the door for a few minutes before heading out, straightening out my clothes and adjusting my hair until it's all perfect. I might not like myself as a person, but I do like the way I look. Ever since I found my style, I've felt a whole lot better about being perceived in general. There's no way I would've let Tasha take pictures of me back in early high school, much less put them all over the internet and show them off at a campus event.

When I make it to the student union, I'm expecting Max to stand out with his head looming over everyone, but the first person I catch sight of is actually Mickey James, noticeable because he's standing with a bunch of guys that look like hockey players through and through, taking up so much space with their energy alone. They're all wearing these nice, tailored suits, holding themselves like they're used to the pageantry. Mickey does have his sleeves rolled up, showing off a fresh tattoo of the purple and black Royals crown on his left forearm, just under the crook of his elbow.

He looks happy. Smiling in a way I've never seen him while his teammates laugh around him. And holy shit, he looks even shorter with them towering above him. It's kind of adorable.

I take a step in his direction and stop when one of his teammates claps him on the shoulder and gives him a strong shake that makes him bust out laughing. It's the floral print of the guy's undershirt that catches my attention. Draws my gaze up to his face, where I get an eyeful of Luca Cicero's big goofy grin.

He didn't catch me rifling through his things, but it still makes me hesitate. What if he saw me and Max stalking away from his study carrel, or someone else watched me go through his bag and told him when he got back? I won't kid myself into thinking I can fistfight a hockey player and come away with all my teeth.

Mickey notices me staring before I can decide whether to run for my life or not, Jaysen standing at his elbow. He smiles at me, motioning me over with a tilt of his head.

I don't bother trying to slip into that paper-thin disguise now that I know just how badly I was pulling it off all along. That would be embarrassing.

Still, when I say, "Mickey James," it comes out as a drawl like it's natural to me.

Mickey gives me an upward nod. "Nathaniel. Didn't think you'd be here."

I slip my hands into the pockets of my slacks, pin my shoulders back a little. "I'm a guest of honor."

He looks at me curiously, but before he can say anything else, Jaysen cuts in. "Hey, so are we."

Mickey rolls his eyes. "A couple of our teammates are showing a documentary they've been making about us all year."

"Documentary," Jaysen echoes with a snort. "It's a sitcom."

"Mockumentary, to be exact," Luca Cicero adds. I can't

look at him directly as he speaks, but there's no hint of animosity in his voice. If anything, he seems amused.

I clear my throat and try not to look so suspicious. "Sounds like this'll be more fun than I anticipated."

"It'll be agonizing, actually," Mickey says.

Jaysen chuckles, resting his elbow on Mickey's shoulder as he looks me over. "What're you a guest of honor for?"

I lean my weight back on one of my heels and cock my head to the side in a semblance of a confident pose. "I'm a model, clearly."

He quirks an eyebrow. "Clearly."

Mickey shakes his head, rolling his eyes once more even as he smiles. He steps behind Jaysen to put his hands on his waist and pushes him along with the crowd starting to move farther into the student union. He meets my eyes and says, "Clearly."

Luca Cicero and the others watch them get a few steps away before looking at me like they're waiting for me to say something. I blink back at them and point in the direction Jaysen and Mickey went.

"I'm gonna . . . ," I trail off, and step into the crowd.

The main room is split up into temporary cubicles, each displaying a different artist's work. I find my friends toward the middle, Tasha's booth set up in a prime location for foot traffic.

They're dressed up just as nice as everyone else here, so

I guess Tasha's instruction was a lot less about me personally and just the overall vibe of the event.

"You look so nice!" Tasha says, grabbing on to my arm once I'm in reach and tugging me into the cubicle. "Come see!"

The outside chatter of the crowd is instantly muffled by the soundproofed walls and the enclosed space. It's almost a surreal experience, stepping into the quiet and seeing . . . me.

I'm not the only person featured in the photos pinned to the walls—there's a few of Max and Celeste and some other people I don't recognize—but I am in most of them. The first time Tasha took pictures of me, it felt like a fashion shoot, but that's not how the photos came out. They're all so artsy, like they're from a coffee table photography book. I'm not looking at the camera in any of them, or even posed really. Like they chose only candids.

Smaller photos are staggered around a huge print in the center of the back wall. Me sitting on the log in the woods with my knees drawn up, arms draped over the top of them. Staring into the water, jaw slack.

Looking completely lost.

I think this might be the most honest depiction of me I've ever seen. Strip away all the grinning and grandstanding and falsehoods, and this is what's left.

I've been trying to figure out who I am—well, this is it.

Completely lost.

Tasha stands by my side, letting me take it all in silently for a few minutes before they say, "What do you think?"

"You're incredible, Tasha," I say. My voice is thick with emotion, which probably seems conceited of me, getting emotional looking at pictures of myself.

Tasha hooks their arm through mine and smiles up at me anyway. "Having a good subject helps."

"No." I shake my head, never looking away from that photo. "This is all you."

They squeeze my arm, leaning their head on my shoulder. In this moment, I feel just a little less lost.

WATCHING PEOPLE FAWN OVER Tasha's pictures of me gives me a better rush than committing crimes ever did.

It even *feels* healthier. Like it's going to linger and I won't crash hard later.

I wouldn't say I'm happy, exactly. Not when I keep looking at that photo and seeing myself for what I really am. But I feel good.

After, the four of us head to the Throne Room for fries. Tasha sits sideways in the booth with their legs across my lap. Celeste and Max crack one deadpan joke after another. I still feel good.

Tasha keeps their arm looped through mine as we walk back to our building. It feels pretty natural, with the way we've been in contact for most of the night, but once Max and Celeste are gone and it's just the two of us, the touching gets my heart racing.

It's like anxiety, but not the painful, dagger-sharp, electrifying kind. More like . . .

Anticipation?

Anticipation for what, though?

"Hey," I say as we step through the back door into our building. "Thank you."

Tasha squeezes their arm around mine, looking up at me with that extra bright smile of theirs. "For what?"

I shrug my shoulders, stopping us at the bottom of the stairwell. I speak softly so my voice doesn't echo all the way up to my roommate. "For tonight. Making me feel important."

They step directly in front of me, unlinking our arms to put their hands on my elbows. The look they give me then is so freaking earnest.

"You *are* important, Nathaniel."

This feels like one of those moments in a movie where everything comes together. Epiphanies are had and changes are made and everything settles down from here.

It feels like the moment where I should kiss them. A real kiss. Not whatever that was we did in their room all those weeks ago.

But I can't. I don't want to. Not yet. Maybe not ever. Probably some time.

Instead, I put my hand gently around their wrist. Hold on to them while they hold on to me.

I swallow, but my voice is still rough when I say, "I know."

Tasha smiles and pulls me in for a bracing hug. I wrap my arms around their shoulders and hold them tightly to me.

This . . . this is something I can do.

CHAPTER 24

MONDAY, I WAKE UP to a text from my mom. She never texts me. If she has something to say, she calls, so I can hear the disappointment in her voice.

I curl my knees to my chest and let my thumb hover over the notification until the screen dims, then finally suck it up and click through to the message.

Mother.
Don't forget, cousin Anita's wedding
is Saturday.

The room spins for a moment, I sit up so fast, and for a second I'm convinced the ringing from my phone is all in my head. Mom picks up, but it's silent for several beats before a sigh comes through, and she says *hello*.

"I'm not going to that wedding," I blurt out, breathless.

I can picture her rubbing her forehead, already getting a migraine from this conversation.

"Yes, you are," she says, her tone daring me to argue.

"Why? Why do I have to be there? It's not like I'm an important member of the family."

"Everyone is expecting you."

I stumble out of bed, a blanket tangling around my legs and almost sending me to the floor. I kick it off my ankles and thread my fingers into my hair and start pacing a circle in the middle of the room.

"I can't go. I'm sick or something. Very contagious—don't want to infect the whole family, y'know?"

"Nathaniel—"

"And I have, like, so much homework. You want me to get good grades, right?"

"Basta."

I clamp my mouth shut. She only tends to slip into Italian when she's about 1,000 percent done with something. Usually me.

"You'll be home the whole week of spring break," she says. "You can work on homework then."

"Mom, seriously, I would rather jump out a window than go to this wedding."

"You're being ridiculous. It's one night. You don't even have to talk to anyone other than Nonna. Everyone is always asking after you. It will be good for them to see that you're doing well."

I sink back onto the edge of my mattress, tilting my head back to sigh at the ceiling. It's not that she assumes I'm doing well. It's her way of telling me I better put on an act. Normal hair. No chains, no makeup, no nail polish. No dramatics. Mom wants everyone to think I'm rehabilitated, done being an embarrassment and ready to make her proud. It's bad enough that she married a criminal—she doesn't need her son carrying on that legacy.

If anyone in my family has actually been asking after me, it's because they're expecting an entertaining story about one fucked-up thing I've done or another.

"Are you listening?" Mom demands when I'm quiet for too long. I mumble something incoherent to let her know I'm still here. "Okay, well, Dad will be there to pick you up Friday afternoon, after your last class. Your brother even managed to get leave for this. It will be nice for us all to be together for a few days."

I breathe out an incredulous laugh. "Nice. Yeah."

That's the last thing I remember saying. I don't remember saying goodbye, or hanging up, but between one breath and the next, I'm lying back on my bed, feet still on the floor, with my phone held against my chest.

Anita is a cousin on my mom's side of the family. She's, like, the same age as my uncle. They're friends with each other. He'd be there anyway, but with their relationship the way it is, he'll probably be in the wedding party. I'll have to look right at him as he stands up there the whole time. Sits at the main table. Probably makes a speech.

I can't do this. I can't go to this wedding. I can't be in the same building as him, let alone in the same room. Just thinking about it makes my heart feel like it's splitting open, on the verge of rupture.

It's one thing after another for me, isn't it? Fall semester went too smoothly and now everything has to come crashing down on me all at once. Like one big *gotcha* moment.

I feel like I should be crying. Like I need to.

My arms are leaden when I lift my hands to my face. Press the heels of my hands hard into my eyes. *Will* myself to cry. I need the release of emotion. Get it out of my system now, bleed myself dry so it doesn't build up to a boiling point later, in front of everyone.

But I can't.

I can't cry, just like I can't breathe, just like I can't function.

I'm spiraling.

I think I'm spiraling.

CHAPTER 25

I ALMOST LEAVE MY building without shoes.

I take one step out the door, and as soon as my bare foot hits the cold, damp concrete stairs, I wake up. Like I wasn't piloting my own body until that moment.

Where am I even going? What the fuck am I doing?

I pull my foot back inside. Let the door slam shut.

Maybe I should go see Tasha.

I can get over what happened to me if only I can step over this one major hurdle. I shouldn't let the actions of someone else define me, keep me from doing something I swear I want to do. I want to touch someone, and I want them to touch me. I want us both to like it. Tasha is interested. It will be fine.

If I can build up the nerve, do this, I'll be okay. Everything will be okay. I can put the past where it belongs.

Right?

Right.

I head back upstairs. The texture on the stairs is rough.

Keeps people from slipping as they carry their lives up and down four flights at the beginning and end of each semester. Gives them a boost when they're late to class and forgot their homework on their desk on the top floor.

It hurts my bare feet.

I get back to my room. Think about sending a message to Tasha. Something to let them know exactly what I want without being rude or gross about it.

But.

No.

It wouldn't be fair to them.

And it wouldn't even work. Hook up with someone to bury my issues? Fuck. It would only make things worse.

God.

I hate this.

This isn't fair. I don't deserve to live like this, to feel like this. Gianna doesn't deserve it. How do I fix us?

How do I fix *me*?

I shove my feet into my Vans, crushing down the backs of them. I stand there for a long while, blinking at the wall, and then I head back out.

People stare at me as I trudge across campus, down toward the north road. Look at me and my half-worn shoes, my sleep-stale joggers and tangled hair. They think I'm finally losing it. I've been unstable since I stepped foot on campus in August and I've finally tipped over the edge and it's nothing but entertainment for them.

Fuck them.

I'm fixing this. I'm fixing myself. I'm not going to keep them entertained any longer.

I almost tear the door off its hinges when I reach the medical center. The older woman at the desk startles. I watch her try to recover as I stop just inside. A welcoming smile flickers across her mouth until she gets a good look at me. Her face pales. She tucks a loose strand of curled blond hair behind her ear, standing slowly as her other hand creeps toward the desk phone.

"Can I help you?" Her voices trembles. What do people usually come to a campus clinic for? Common colds, twisted ankles, the morning-after pill? Probably not full-on nervous breakdowns like this.

I take a moment to collect myself. I'm not here to scare the shit out of this poor receptionist. I'm here for help. I comb my fingers through my hair, snagging on knots. Tug my sleeves over my fingertips when I'm done.

"I need to speak to a counselor," I say, breathless. "Please."

She seems to relax, just a bit, when I don't take another step forward. Her hand still hovers near the phone.

"Do you have an appointment?"

"No. It's—it's an . . ."

"You'll need to make an appointment, dear." Her voice no

longer shakes. Now it's soothing. Like I'm a wild animal she's trying to keep calm. "There are no openings today."

My fingers curl against my chest, bunching in the fabric of my hoodie. "It's an emergency."

She blinks at me, lips pursing. The room is too quiet. I can hear my pulse in my eardrums. Feel it pumping through the backs of my hands, too fast, too hard. It makes me want to scratch my skin open.

"If it's an emergency," she says carefully, with trained composure, "I can call for an ambulance."

"No." I take a desperate step forward, and she flinches back. "No. I don't need the hospital. I just need to talk to someone."

"Then I can set up an appointment for you, or you can make one online through your student portal."

"When's the soonest I can get in?"

The receptionist lowers herself back into her chair, keeping her eyes on me until she's ready to look at her computer screen. She clicks a few times, frowning in concentration.

"For a new psychiatry patient, the next opening I have is . . . April twenty-sixth."

"That's like almost a month away."

She winces. "It's always busy at this point in the semester."

"I can't wait that long."

Muted footsteps on the carpet behind me make me jump. I whip around to find Mickey James standing at my elbow. Two other students sit in the waiting area I didn't bother to check as I came in, watching me have a meltdown with passive curiosity.

"He can have my appointment slot," Mickey says.

The receptionist shakes her head. "He's a new patient. There's paperwork. The doctors take more time with them. It won't fit."

"Who cares about paperwork or time? He needs help."

"And I can call him an ambulance."

I walk out.

One of my shoes slides off my foot as I step off the curb. I almost trip on my next step, and then I'm sitting. On the damp cement of the curb with my forehead pressed into my knees and fingers laced against the back of my skull, hair trapped between them, pinching.

I hold my breath until I can't.

The door of the medical center squeals open as the air leaves me in a rush. I suck it back in as someone sits down beside me.

Quiet, until Mickey says, "You can talk to me, if you want."

I try to shake my head, but it's pinned too tightly between my knees and my hands.

"No," I breathe. "No, I—what are you even doing here? Sprain your ankle on the ice? Lose a tooth? Concussion?"

"Therapy," he says plainly. "Depression."

I let it sink in. Mickey James. Mickey James with his talent and his fame and his fortune. Mickey James with his depression.

I squeeze my eyes shut. Is he another one like me and Gianna?

"What do you have to be depressed about?" I mutter.

He breathes in slowly. I feel him move beside me. Hear his shoes scrape against loose rocks in the road as he stretches out his legs.

"Nothing, really," he says. "I just am."

I laugh. It comes out as this strangled wheeze. If someone with nothing to be depressed about can still be depressed, then what hope do I have?

"You should still make an appointment," Mickey says when I offer nothing more than that laugh. "People cancel. They could get you in sooner. And like I said. You can talk to me. I probably won't know what to say like a therapist would, but sometimes it helps just to talk at someone. Venting, you know?"

I stay quiet, but Mickey doesn't leave me. My stomach roils, little surges of nauseated anxiety as my heart flitters like the wings of a hummingbird. Each breath is its own little gasp.

I came here to talk to someone. Mickey's no professional therapist, but he sees one himself. And he's here and he's

willing and if he goes telling everyone what I say, well . . .
I guess it doesn't really matter.

My fingers loosen on the back of my skull. I forcibly relax
my shoulders. Sit up slowly, eyes closed as I tilt my head back.
I inhale long, slow, controlled, and open my eyes. The sky
is bright, bright blue. The faintest wisps of clouds drift lazily
past the sun. It's so beautiful it looks almost fake.

Beside me, Mickey waits patiently.

When I open my mouth, it's not my fears about the wedding waiting on my tongue.

"I can't see myself in the future," I say. My voice is a
monotone. "I don't think I belong there. I can't see myself
having a life. Being anything but a side character in everyone else's stories. I'm like an extra in a movie, doing something ridiculous in the background while the real people
live real lives. I don't know why I'm here. What's the point
of me?"

Mickey rolls and unrolls the cuff on the left sleeve of his
sweater. It's too big for him. One of his curls falls into his
eyes and he brushes it away before going right back to fid-
geting with his sleeve.

It takes him a while to speak.

"You belong in the future, Nathaniel. You have plenty
of time to figure out what your place there is and what you
want your story to be." He takes a small breath. "And it's okay

to just . . . to just live. You're a person and you're living and that's why you're here. That's the point. To just live."

"What if I don't want to?" I whisper to the clouds.

He's quiet even longer this time. I feel bad. Dumping that on him when he's already dealing with his own shit. That's the kind of thing that makes you panic. Makes you feel like you have someone's life in your hands.

But then he says, softly, delicately, "When I start feeling like that, I try to think of all the things I would hate to miss if I died. Like, I would hate to miss my sisters' graduations. The day my niece is born. The day the Sabres finally win the goddamn Stanley Cup. Winning it myself. Playing against my friends in the NHL. They don't have to be big things like that, either. I would really hate to miss the next crepe day in the dining hall. Dorian and Barbie in the drag show in a couple weeks. Anything to give you the motivation to hold on."

I close my eyes again. What would I hate to miss? What do I have to hold on for?

Nothing. The answer is nothing, because I am nothing.

I exist.

I only exist.

"Does that help?" Mickey asks.

I nod. I say thank you. Because I don't want him to feel bad. I'm sure his advice would work for anyone other than me.

He texts himself with my phone so we have each other's numbers. He sits with me until I'm ready to leave.

When I get back to my room, a message is waiting for me.

Mickey
When you have an answer,
I want to hear it.
I would hate to miss it:

CHAPTER 26

MY FRIENDS ARE EXTRA busy with lacrosse this week, traveling for a couple away games, so it's easy to sink into myself without them to tell me to cut it out. I sit in bed with my laptop refreshing the scores on their team pages and mastering a particularly tricky card flourish, involved enough to keep my mind from wandering to this weekend or my childhood or how they both overlap.

I don't realize I've fucked up until I walk into class on Thursday.

I'm scheduled to give my speech today, and I never reworked my outline.

My backpack falls into the crook of my elbow as I make an anguished face at the ceiling. I let the strap drop into my fingers, then fall to the floor.

It's the kind of dramatics people expect from me. I feel like crumpling to my knees, curling up on my side right in the doorway.

I pick up my backpack and leave the room. Don't stop

when Celeste calls my name from our table. Keep my chin tucked when Professor Huang says, "Mr. Conti?" as I pass her in the hall.

I'm going to fail this class. No point sitting through it.

I don't know where I go, how I pass the time till my next class, but when I get there, the professor starts handing out a midterm packet that I had no idea was coming. Reading through the questions, I have to double-check I'm in the right room, with the right people. Nothing makes sense. I slip my phone out of my pocket and type the terms into Google under the table.

Professor Loren clears his throat. I don't even look at him. I close my eyes, press my phone against my thigh, and stand to follow him down the hall to his office. He makes me sit there while he files an Honor Code violation against me. I offer no explanation or apology.

I don't have the energy to speak.

I scribble some semblance of my name on the line at the bottom of the page he prints out, and wander back to my room. I kick my shoes off at the edge of my bed and crawl under the blankets in my normal clothes.

I lie there, unmoving, knees pulled to my chest, eyes blurred from staring at the same spot where my blankets bunch up then disappear between the wall and the mattress.

Sometimes I sleep. And when I'm not sleeping, I wish I could be.

Sleep feels nice because it feels like nothing.

There's hushed voices behind me. Scottie. Max.

Max sits on the edge of my bed and puts a hand on my shoulder. Tries to roll me onto my back, get me to look at him. I come alive only enough to resist him. Turn my face further into the pillow.

He leaves. Comes back later with Tasha and Celeste.

Tasha is nice. I can tell by the soft tone of their voice. But they're always nice.

Celeste tries to be nice at first. Then she gets frustrated. She kneels on my mattress, leans over me so her hair falls onto my hands curled in front of my chest.

"Get out of bed."

She hooks her fingers into the top of the blanket where it's pulled tight against my shoulder and tugs. I let her pull it off of me. I'm still in the clothes I wore to class. I don't know how long ago that was.

"Nathaniel." Celeste's voice is stern, like a professor handing back tests she's disappointed in.

She goes to move me with a hand on my shoulder, like Max did this morning, or yesterday, or days ago, and I don't fight it this time. I don't want to. I can't.

I flop onto my back. Stare blankly up at the ceiling. Like a corpse. Celeste's fingers dig into my jaw when she forces my face to turn toward her.

"This is dramatic even for you," she says. "Enough."

Her words are harsh, but all I see in her eyes is concern. I blink at her, let my vision come into focus for the first time in hours to take in the tension between her eyebrows, the fearful intensity in her eyes.

Behind her, Tasha's hands are folded in front of their mouth, tears tracking down their cheeks, and Max has a hand fisted into the swoop of hair off his forehead.

Scottie's gone.

But these three. These three care about me. They don't know what's wrong with me or what's happened, but it worries them. It scares them.

I don't deserve it. I don't deserve their worry or their care. Not when I left my cousin to suffer alone.

I close my eyes.

I don't deserve their pity and I don't deserve my own.

"What's going on, Nat?"

"Please go," I say. I try to say. I don't know if anything makes it out with the way my throat is closing.

"You can talk to us. We're here for you."

I don't want them to be. I'm fucking everything up. I'll only drag them down with me, the way I've always done with Max.

"Just go."

This time, I know the words make it past my teeth. I feel them scrape up my throat, raw and exhausting and final.

I don't know how long it takes them to listen. I don't

open my eyes again until my phone rings. My dad, here to pick me up.

As we drive off campus, I rest my head against the window and look up at the bell tower. The library at the top of the hill with its glass walls and brick and black supports. The woods beyond that, a few trees sporting impatient buds.

It feels like the last time I'll see any of it.

CHAPTER 27

DAD DOESN'T SPEAK UNTIL we hit the highway a half hour into our two-hour drive. He asks me why I look like I haven't showered in days.

"Because I haven't," I say.

He pauses. "Did you go to class like that?"

"No."

He inhales sharply through his mouth like he's prepping to tear into me, but that's always been a team effort between him and Mom, so he holds back for now. Turns the radio up on his Canadian rock station and leaves me to silently stare out the window as the distance between me and every shitty thing that's happened to me closes by the minute.

My family didn't always despise me. I was perfectly pleasant as a small child. Well-behaved and well-mannered and well-liked, until everything *well* about me was stolen by a piece of shit teenager who got away with it. My parents didn't know what had changed, so they didn't know how to fix it.

Nothing they did or said had an impact. They raised me and Seth exactly the same and he came out perfectly, so it must have been a failure of character on my part. Something unmendable.

They gave up on me a long time ago. Any parenting they do now is out of obligation.

It's raining when we pull into the driveway at home. A light mist, barely noticeable on the skin as I haul myself out of Dad's car. I stand with one hand on the door and one on the roof of the car and tilt my head to the sky, let the mist settle on my face.

I can make it through this. I can survive this weekend and make it back to campus and fix everything I've fucked up in the past week. I can be here without actually being here, and I can come out on the other side untouched.

I will be okay.

And if I'm not, well, it's nothing new.

The house is a small two-bedroom with a tiny galley-style kitchen and one cramped bathroom. There will be nowhere for me to go to get away from my family. No space to breathe. The front door opens right into the living room where Mom is always curled up in the corner of the couch knitting and watching soap operas, so as soon as I walk in, I'm gonna be in for it. Dad leaves the door open, not expecting me to hesitate outside.

Celeste would call this dramatic, having to brace myself to walk into my own, perfectly normal house with its perfectly normal occupants. I'm the thing that makes this family unstable. But if I'm going to get through this, I need to take every measure to keep myself steady, no matter how dramatic it might be.

I stand up tall. Square my shoulders and roll my neck from side to side to loosen it up. Shake out my hands and bounce on my toes and arrange my face into a blank, neutral canvas.

One deep breath, and I step inside.

Mom is on the couch, right where I expected to find her, but so is Riley, my sister-in-law, which means Seth is already here somewhere too.

It's the first blow to my manufactured calm, and I feel the tether start to fray. I blink hard and shake my head to keep myself here. I figured, being in the navy and all, he'd only show up like an hour before the wedding and have to leave halfway through. I didn't prepare myself to see him today.

Mom and Riley go quiet when I walk in. I step out of my shoes. Push them under the bench by the door and hope Mom doesn't notice the small smudge of mud they leave on the gray vinyl flooring. When I look up again, Riley is off the couch and stepping toward me with a cautious smile, opening her arms as if to hug me.

"It's good to see you, Nathaniel," she says.

I stare blankly at her, then look over her shoulder at Mom, who looks back at me like I'm a disgrace. I take that to mean I should probably hug my sister-in-law. She's so . . . wispy. From her floaty blond hair to the way her arms don't feel like they're actually touching me when she puts them around me. I don't think I actually touch her either. We're both hugging the air around each other like we don't know why we're doing it to begin with.

Because we're family now, and families are supposed to hug.

Seth comes in from the small hallway leading to the bathroom and bedrooms just as Riley steps away from me. He stops short, like he's not exactly sure of what he just witnessed, before he lifts his eyebrows and shakes his head in bewilderment, brushing it off.

"Hey," he says.

He's definitely toned up since I saw him last. He always worked out and kept that same military haircut, but it always looked like a costume on him before. Now it looks real.

By the time I realize I should probably say something, it's been too long, too awkward, and I can't gather up the energy to start a conversation I don't want to have to begin with. I head to the room I shared with Seth without a word, all three of them watching me go. As I turn into the hallway, Mom finally speaks up.

"Riley's going to dye your hair tonight."

There's never been much of me in mine and Seth's room. He has sensible, boring tastes that our parents were willing to work with, while they probably assumed I'd turn the room into some kind of dungeon or rave pit.

The light grayish-blue walls were his choice. The off-white carpet. The beige desk that looks like it's out of a professor's office, the matching dresser. Mom and Dad said it was because he was older, that when he moved out, I could do what I wanted with the room.

It didn't come up again after he left for the Navy and I knew better than to ask about it. There's no way they'd let me mess with Seth's room.

Every wall is filled up with framed awards, *Seth A. Conti* written in fancy script, honoring his academic achievements, his contributions to the community, his mere existence. My sophomore year lacrosse MVP trophy is lost among his track medals and old science projects. Mom and Dad's pride for Seth fills them so completely, it leaves no room for me.

Honestly, I'm surprised they even remembered I existed to force me to come to this wedding. They usually like to pretend they only have one son.

I drop my bag onto the floor by the bunk bed and duck

into the bottom bunk. The only part of this room that's mine, with the random dark artwork taped to the small patch of wall, printed out on computer paper in my high school library. The relatable song lyrics scratched into the underside of Seth's bunk, pen holes stabbed through the cardboard when I needed to take my feelings out on something other than myself.

Now, I run my fingers over all that evidence of my own misery and wonder where I'd be now if only I'd had a healthy childhood. I don't even remember who I was as a kid. What I wanted to be when I grew up. What I liked, what I obsessed over. I look back on my childhood and all that's there is guilt and shame.

I pull my hand away from the shredded cardboard and rest it on my chest, feel my heartbeat under my fingertips, still going despite all the times I wished it would stop.

I made it through the past couple years because I was convinced things would get better with distance and time. I'd go to college and I'd find myself and my people and everything would be fine.

Maybe things will never be fine, but they can at least be better.

I take out my phone and send a message to Mickey.

I would hate to never see Hartland again.

An hour later, I'm sitting on the closed toilet lid while Riley massages black dye into the white half of my hair.

It feels degrading, especially with Seth sitting on the edge of the bathtub and laughing with his wife as if she's not actively taking away one of the few things I like about myself.

I scrub off my black nail polish while waiting for the dye to set and rinse my hair in the shower until it goes cold, and then I stand under the freezing water without really feeling it until Dad knocks on the door and shouts about dinner being ready.

When I sit at the cramped, round table in a corner of the kitchen, I still haven't said a word since I've been home. I don't remember the last time I ate, so the smell of Dad's chili makes my stomach churn. I breathe shallowly, sitting far back in my chair and keeping my eyes on the wall. I can only ever stomach fries or toast when I get like this, not some heavy-ass chili.

There's a new shelf on the wall above the table. It wasn't there when I was home over the semester break. A succulent in a marbled pot sits on the left side. On the right, a stack of three books with blank spines. In the middle, a picture frame that says *Family* along the bottom holding a wedding photo, taken on the steps to a gazebo outside the church where Seth and Riley got married. The two of them holding hands in the center, flanked on one side by Riley's parents and ours on the other. I'm there, but it's clear that I'm separate. Standing a step or two away from Dad while everyone else is gathered in close, my smile a mimicry of theirs.

Distantly, I know someone just said my name. But I can't take my eyes off that photo. Family.

They could've easily cropped me out, excused it because it's a wedding photo. But I'm still there. Included at a distance.

Family.

I've spent the past however many days feeling nothing at all, but now . . . now I just feel a little sad.

"Nathaniel?" they try again. Mom this time.

I blink slowly back into my body and turn my head to look at her.

"Your brother asked you a question."

My eyes slide over to Seth.

There's a beat of silence before he says, "How's school going? You haven't told me anything."

"You haven't asked," I say. I don't know why the responsibility to contact him is on me, when he's the one in the navy with the strict schedule and shit he's not allowed to talk about. When he's the older brother. I've called him once, and how many times has he called me?

None.

I don't say it with an attitude. In fact, there's barely any inflection in my voice at all, but the way the table implodes with my words, you'd think I stabbed him rather than pointed out a basic fact.

"Can't you just answer the question without being antagonistic?" Dad demands.

I scoop up a spoonful of chili and let it plop back into the bowl. "I wasn't."

"I'd like to hear the answer too," Mom says, resting an arm on the table and leaning in closer, face tight with anger or disappointment or hatred, or maybe all three. "You don't go to class, so I'm sure you're having a great time."

"I go to class."

"I would hope so, or else you'll have all that debt without a degree to show for it."

"Should've put some community college apps in front of me," I say. "Instead of all the most expensive private schools in the state."

"You had the grades for it, Nathaniel!" Dad says. He doesn't even sound angry anymore. Just exasperated. "You could do so much if you just put in the effort!"

"I'm sure you could have too," I mutter. "If you weren't in a cell your senior year."

He slams his fist on the table so hard, silverware rattles, and everyone else flinches. Dad stares into his bowl, taking slow, measured breaths. He shakes his head and speaks through his teeth. "Why are you trying so hard to take after me?"

I open my mouth to argue. To say that I'm not. That at least I'm in school, at least I haven't gotten arrested lately, *at least at least at least*. But Dad pushes himself to his feet, hands pressing hard against the table for support, and my mouth hangs silently open.

When did Dad start looking so tired and old?

I watch, dumbfounded, as he leaves the table, dragging his feet, and disappears through the kitchen. I can hear Riley's shallow breathing next to me, like she's making an effort to go unnoticed. That we did this in front of her means she really is part of the family.

Mom crumples a napkin in her hand, taking a deep breath before she says, "You need to stop holding that over him, Nathaniel." She holds a hand up to stop me when I scoff, like she knows exactly what I'm thinking. "Wanting you to be better than him does not make him a hypocrite."

Riley quietly excuses herself. I expect Seth to follow her, but he stays, and when I glance over at him, the corner of his mouth quirks up into the barest hint of a sympathetic smile, like he's sorry for starting this whole thing. I quickly look back to my bowl of chili. I can't handle some kind of brotherly moment on top of everything else right now.

Mom doesn't say anything else. She silently gathers up the abandoned bowls from the table, rinses them in the sink, loads them into the dishwasher.

I'd rather she be raging at me. I'd rather Dad come back

and start yelling. I need the familiar anger, the conversations I could block out entirely but still write a play-by-play on without hearing a word.

I don't know what to do with this tired disappointment.

It almost makes me feel like I really am the problem.

CHAPTER 28

I BARELY SLEEP THAT night. I'm too aware of Seth and Riley in the bunk above me. Too afraid of what's going to happen at this wedding. Too conscious of Mom and Dad's utter contempt for my existence.

I lie awake with the sound of Riley's soft snoring and the blinking light of someone's unopened phone notification flashing on the walls, and when morning comes, I'm too tired to panic.

Dad makes bacon, which my empty stomach can handle in small nibbles, so that takes care of one thing. I stare at myself in the mirror as I brush my teeth, and I hate the thing looking back at me. The washed-out pallor of my skin, the yellowed bruises under my eyes. The all-black hair is fine really, but it's just not me at this point. I look like a sickly, watered-down version of myself, and it only gets worse when I pull on the denim jeans and baby blue button-down Mom laid out for me.

Anita's getting married in a barn, with a dress code that only Seth gets to break in his fancy Navy uniform.

I'm sitting at the desk in our room, pushing gel through my hair with my fingers to find something of myself in my face when Seth comes in. He softly closes the door behind him, and that paired up with the serious look on his face gets my attention. I sit up straighter, shoulders pinned to the chair's backrest, and eye him with suspicion as he leans against the dresser next to the desk. He doesn't look at me directly, and I keep my mouth shut until he builds up the nerve to say what he came in here to say.

Which is: "Are you okay, Nathaniel?"

I blink up at him a few times before facing the mirror again, frowning as I put the finishing touches on my hair.

"What do you mean, am I okay?" I mutter.

He crosses his arms, looks down at his feet as he shifts his weight against the dresser, clearly uncomfortable. "You look awful."

I scoff, motioning to my farmhouse outfit. "Of course I do. The country boy aesthetic doesn't suit me."

"That's not what I mean. I mean . . ." He sighs. "Look, I know we haven't been close in . . . in a while, but I have been paying attention. Mom and Dad want to believe you're just being difficult to spite them because they don't want to think they went wrong somewhere. But it's deeper than that, isn't it?"

I stand up from the desk, wiping my hands on the towel I used after showering last night. "If you really think so, why don't you go talk to them about it?"

"Because I'm worried about you. One of my shipmates . . . his brother killed himself a few weeks ago, and the way he talked about him leading up to it, it . . . well, it made me think of you."

I go completely still. I feel cold. It starts in my fingertips and creeps up my arms until it hits my heart and I don't think it beats again after that.

First Max.

Then Celeste.

Now Seth.

"Why does everyone think I'm going to kill myself?"

Seth hikes his shoulders up, tightening his arms around himself. It's the closest thing to insecurity I've ever seen on him. "Are you?"

I turn my back on him, balling up the towel to shove it into the dirty clothes hamper. "I don't have it written in my daily to-do list, no."

The dresser creaks as he pushes off of it, stepping closer to me. My whole body tenses.

"Nathaniel, please," he says. The desperation is clear in his voice. Less clear is what exactly he's desperate for. "I'm sorry I wasn't a good brother to you when we were kids, but I don't want to lose you. Can we start over?"

I slowly turn to face him again, keeping my voice as calm and unaffected as possible, even as this unfamiliar feeling flickers to life in my chest. Something like hope. "Where?" I ask. "Where do we start over from, Seth? Where do you think it went wrong?"

We look each other in the eye, and a part of me wants him to come right out and say it. To make the connection between that phone call I made from the library and all of my issues. I want him to say that he knows what happened to me and that he's sorry he didn't protect me or defend me, but I don't even know if that's true. I don't think he does know, but I want him to. I don't want to be alone with this knowledge anymore.

"I don't know," he says, and my hope fizzles. "I don't know what's wrong or why, but I want us to be good. I want you to be good."

"I'm good."

Seth lets out a slow breath and I watch him slump in palpable disappointment. But it's not like Mom and Dad's disappointment in me. It's like he's disappointed in himself.

Guilt simmers in my chest. I feel it starting to burn through my blood.

"May—maybe we can . . . we can . . . ," I try, but it comes out all disjointed and unsure and I have to pause to figure out what I really want to say before a bunch of nonsense blurts out of my mouth. Seth waits expectantly, eyebrows pinched up in hopeful expectation. "Sure. We can start over. Maybe video chat once a week or something. You can let me in on all your government secrets and I'll complain about homework."

His head pulls back in surprise, which only makes me feel more guilty.

"Yeah," he says, excitement clear in his voice. "That'd be awesome. I'll make sure it's a secure line."

Now it's my turn to be surprised. Did he just make a joke?

I tilt my head to the side, eyes narrowed as I look him over and huff out a laugh. Maybe my brother isn't as bad as I thought. It would've been nice for him to speak up for me every once in a while, when Mom and Dad were using him as a measuring stick for me, but I won't call this too little too late.

We'll never be best friends or anything like that, but this feels good.

He sways forward slightly, like he's going to take a step toward me and thinks better of it, and rubs the back of his head sheepishly.

"Don't you dare hug me," I say, catching on.

Seth laughs, and even I smile, just a little.

CHAPTER 29

IF THERE WAS EVER a time I wish I knew how to dissociate on command, it's now.

I've seen people talk about being able to do it. Seen the videos making light of it. But no one ever explains how they do it.

I guess that's probably for the best.

None of the wedding party is around when we show up, which should be enough to calm at least some of my nerves, if it weren't for how I know my family views me.

I already feel their eyes on me and I've barely stepped foot into this barn. I hide behind Seth and Riley and try to tell myself they're looking at the two of them. At Seth in uniform and Riley in her flowy country dress with her hand on his arm. The perfect, respectable military couple that they are.

But my extended family has always taken far more interest in the fuckups like me than the ones with it all together.

I keep my eyes on the horrible cowboy boots Mom

forced on me, crunching over the hay and white flower pet-
als strewn across the hard-packed dirt floor. It smells like a
corn maze filled with pumpkin spice candles and I don't get
why they didn't have this wedding in October if they wanted
autumn vibes so bad.

Aunt Francesca's shrill voice cuts through the steady rumble of so many people talking in one place, and I flinch as she
comes bounding over to wrap Mom in a hug like she hasn't
seen her in years when I know all of these siblings are in constant contact.

Aunt Francesca is the oldest of Mom's siblings and from
what I've seen, she takes that role very seriously. She's their
staunch protector, defending them against everything and
everyone. Even when the threat comes from among them,
like with Aunt Rosa.

She was so quick to turn on Aunt Rosa.

Seth takes a step back to stand beside me. I can't tell if he
wants to be as far from her as possible too or if he's trying
to show solidarity because he sees the way she's eyeing me.
Maybe he just doesn't want to be used as a hiding spot anymore.

Aunt Francesca moves on to hug Dad, because he's a
reformed fuckup after all, then fawns over Riley for a bit, asking her to spin to show off the way her dress bells out around
her. When Riley is thoroughly blushing with embarrassment,

Aunt Francesca stops in front of Seth and touches the badges on his uniform jacket, asking what they mean.

I turn away after the fourth time I catch her eyes flicking over to me.

This is a literal barn, converted from its original animal-holding purpose to serve as a rustic banquet hall, but still a barn. Wide open, nowhere to hide. There's a detached bathroom outside, but that runs the risk of seeing the groomsmen wandering about, and I need to avoid that as long as I can.

A hand on my elbow makes me jump, and I tug my arm away reflexively. Aunt Francesca holds her hand to her chest like she's the startled one, mouth slightly open on the end of a gasp before she recovers with a smile.

"It's good to see you, Nathaniel," she says. "It's been so long."

I keep my mouth shut, because if I open it, what's going to come out is *I had hoped to never see any of you again.*

Mom is giving me a stern look over Aunt Francesca's shoulder, and Dad looks like he's bracing himself, but I am ready to stand here silently until she gets bored and walks away.

Aunt Francesca barely falters. If anything, an attitude is exactly what she was looking for. It gives her something to gossip about later. She gives me a slow inspection, taking in my clothes and my hair, the sunken look to my eyes. She'll probably tell the whole family I'm on drugs. Try to convince Mom to finally cut the cord, because I'm not worth it.

I go to pick nervously at my nail polish, only to remember I took it off last night. There are no cards in my pockets. Nothing to occupy myself with. My hands curl into fists instead, fingernails digging into my palms.

Aunt Francesca notices the movement, cocking her head to the side. "You're in college now, aren't you? How is that going?"

Mom must see it on my face that I'm going to keep being difficult, because she steps in to say, "He made the dean's list last semester!"

I've never heard such pride in her voice when talking about me. It catches me off guard, makes me do a double take.

It's gotta be fake.

Yeah, I made the dean's list. But it's not like I had bad grades in high school and this was unexpected. I'm good at bullshitting my way to As.

This semester might be a different story. How was I supposed to know Max would reappear in my life and throw everything off?

Seth gives me a little wave to catch my attention as Mom talks with Aunt Francesca about my grades and motions for me to follow him and Riley to one of the round tables where our names are written on little placards to designate our seats. I sit down beside my brother, legs tangling in the white tablecloth hanging all the way to the floor, and start folding and unfolding the sign with my name on it.

Mr. Nathaniel Salvatore Conti.

So formal for a barn wedding.

"That's the worst one out of the way, yeah?" Seth says with a small, cautious smile.

No, I want to say. *Not even close.*

But he's trying and I appreciate it too much to dampen that. So I smile and nod before returning my attention to folding my name card.

My shoulders rise and my chin tucks closer to my chest as more and more of my family show up, individual voices indecipherable within the sound of the crowd. Aunts and uncles and cousins stop by the table to talk to Seth and Riley, but if they say anything to me, I don't notice. My name is a pile of shredded paper on the table by the time Mom and Dad join us, along with Aunt Francesca and a couple cousins, and the rising volume of the music signals the start of the ceremony.

Everything shifts to the background. The music sounds like it's coming from the other side of a door, like I've locked myself in the bathroom at a house party. I hear my own breathing more clearly, harsh and unsteady. I brush my fingers through the remains of my name card, spreading the scraps across the tablecloth in front of me.

I don't look up as the wedding party marches in. I gather the paper back into its tiny pile and sweep it across the table again. Again. Again.

Mom presses my hand onto the table with her own and I snap my head up to look at her. Her jaw is clenched tightly, annoyed, but her eyes are on the ceremony playing out in front of us.

I follow her gaze like I want to be hurt.

I don't recognize him at first. He was fifteen last time I saw him, and now he's twenty-three. I wish the years had done a number on him. I wish the guilt had driven him to the edge like it did to me. I wish I could see misery written all over him.

But he's smiling, watching his niece who's barely younger than him get married, standing in her wedding party. Completely unaffected.

Of course he's unaffected. He got away with it. He was even coddled for it. Made out to be the victim.

I'm going to be sick if I keep sitting here.

I try to leave discreetly, but I'm so close to unraveling, I stand too fast. Knock my chair onto its back legs and have to catch it before it clatters to the ground. The minister hesitates, and I hear everyone turn to look at me more than I see it. Knowing his eyes are on me makes me want to climb out of my own skin.

Mom whispers my name sharply as the minister picks up his speech again.

"Sick," I manage to whisper back, and stagger toward the exit, out into the entryway with its coat racks and the welcome signs and the framed photos of wedding dresses on the walls.

I pace up and down the corridor, chewing on my thumbnail. No one comes to check on me. No one would ever make a scene of themselves to make sure I'm okay.

I need to get out of here. I can't stay here through this ceremony, through the reception, when everyone will be walking around, mingling, looking at me.

I find Dad's light leather jacket hanging from one of the hooks on the wall and dig around for his keys. His pockets are empty except for a crumpled grocery store receipt. I rummage through Mom's instead and find nothing at all. The keys must be in that tiny purse she's carrying with her.

Someone here had to have left their keys in their jacket. I go down the line of them, dropping gum wrappers and receipts and scraps of paper on the floor in my wake. One pocket has a little notepad in it. Another a library card, which I almost mistake for a credit card and pocket myself until I realize what it is. I finally find an overcrowded key ring in the pocket of a pastel pink windbreaker.

I hold them close to my chest as I leave the barn and click the lock button on the key fob, following the chirp to a black Jeep. I don't know who it belongs to. If it's a family member or one of cousin Anita's in-laws or friends, and I don't care.

It's an escape route when I need one most, and I'm not about to pass it up.

CHAPTER 30

MAX AND I USED to talk about all the places we'd go together when we got our driver's licenses. All the trips we'd take and the playlists that would backdrop them.

Max would say famous American cities, like New York, Seattle, and New Orleans, and I would say things like, *into the sea,* or *somewhere no one knows my name,* and *anywhere, just away from here.*

That should have been the first sign.

Max was gone before he could take his driver's test and my parents still haven't let me take mine. We've never driven anywhere together.

The time between getting into the Jeep and pulling onto the Hartland campus is lost to me, but I understand what my subconscious was getting at, bringing me here. Campus is nearly deserted for spring break, only spring athletes and students who live too far to make the travel worth it for a week still here.

I park the car and leave it running as I take out my phone to text Max, Tasha, and Celeste.

im in the woods lot
lets go for a drive

I turn the overhead light on so they'll see me and wait.

The three of them show up together a few minutes later, like they got my message when they were already with each other and ran here right away. Max opens the passenger door, but none of them get in. They stand huddled close together so they can all look at me.

"Where have you been?" Max asks. He's trying to keep his voice gentle and even, like he's afraid to push me over some kind of edge, but he can't fully mask the frustration in his voice.

It stings.

"Wedding," I say, motioning to my clothes. "In a barn. It was awful."

"You didn't think to tell any of us? Or answer our texts? You scared the shit out of us, Nat—we thought you were staying on campus for the break."

"We were about to start calling hospitals," Celeste adds. Tasha is quiet, holding on to their elbows, frowning.

"Can't text at a wedding," I say. "That would be rude. C'mon, I wanna go for a drive. We can go to Auburn, get Taco Bell."

They exchange a look, all three of them, before Max leans into the car, hands on the passenger seat so he can get a closer look at me.

I narrow my eyes. "I'm not drunk. I drove all the way here."

"All right. Can't blame me for being cautious."

He climbs into the car and Celeste and Tasha slowly get into the back seat like they're still not sure about this.

That stings too. I might be terrible and untrustworthy, but I've never given them a reason to think I'm dangerous, have I?

I bite my tongue as I back out of the parking space and head out of the lot, down the hill to the road and turn north toward Auburn.

Max pulls down his visor. Opens the glove box, rifles through the travel packs of tissues and tiny hand sanitizers stored in there. "Whose car is this?"

"Mine," I say, way too quickly. "My parents got it for me . . . for making dean's list last semester."

I see the way he clenches his jaw out of the corner of my eye. He doesn't believe me and he shouldn't, but it still hurts. Even if I knew he was lying to me, I'd act like whatever he said was true until I believed it myself.

I tighten my grip on the steering wheel and press harder on the gas pedal.

Tasha speaks up for the first time when we're about five minutes off campus, saying, "Who got married?"

My lip curls. "One of my many, many cousins. The whole family was there, so my mom dressed me up as the person she wishes I was and crossed her fingers that I wouldn't embarrass her, and then I did anyway by walking out all dramatic-like."

"Slow down, Nat," Max says sternly.

I ease off the gas pedal.

"Why did you walk out?" Celeste asks. I glance at her in the rearview mirror, because she doesn't even sound like she's just looking for gossip. She sounds nervous. She and Tasha are sitting close, holding hands and looking deeply uncomfortable.

I take a deep breath and try to make myself seem calmer for them. I hate that they're afraid of me right now.

"He's happy," I say, turning my eyes back to the road. "He's happy when he doesn't deserve to be, and I'm not. I couldn't sit there and watch him smile like that—I just couldn't."

"Who?" Celeste presses. "Who are you talking about?"

I inhale sharply, and I hear Max do the same, like we're both about to speak, but we can't bring ourselves to utter the words on the tips of our tongues. I feel myself shaking and I think I might shatter myself apart right here in the driver's seat of this stolen Jeep if it doesn't stop soon.

"Slow down, Nat," Max says again, but I barely hear him now.

Why does he get to be happy? Why does he get to steal my happiness, Gianna's happiness, and then carry on like nothing ever happened?

Why are we the ones left suffering the consequences of his actions?

"Nathaniel."

My full name on Max's strained voice snaps me back into the car, my eyes refocusing on the road passing by fast, way too fast. I press hard on the brake pedal, and Celeste swears sharply as we're all rocked forward against our seat belts until I ease off and let us coast.

"Pull over," Max says. He's never talked to me like this before. With anger and worry bleeding into his words in equal measure. Not even when I was asking him to do stupid and illegal things with me. "We can still go to Taco Bell or whatever you want, but I'm driving."

I pull off onto the gravel shoulder without arguing, shame burning in my chest. I keep my head down when I step out to swap seats, but Max stops in my path in front of the car, the headlights shining on us like a spotlight for Celeste and Tasha.

"Did he try to talk to you or something?" Max asks.

I blink up at him. "Huh?"

"You know . . ."

My eyebrows furrow and my lip curls in genuine confusion for a second before I realize.

He knows.

He knows about my uncle. Maybe not what he did, but he knows enough to make the connection. How? I never told him. I never told anyone.

And I don't plan to now.

"I don't know what you're talking about," I say, tucking my shoulder to brush past him. I hear his sigh as I climb into the passenger seat. Max gets in on the driver's side as I click my seat belt into place. "We can go back to campus, I don't care."

"I'll take you to Auburn—it's fine."

"No. I want to take off these stupid clothes. I want to go to bed."

I sink low in the seat, try to tug the sleeves of this awful shirt over my hands, but it's too well-fitted and won't budge.

"You know you can talk to us, right, Nathaniel?" Tasha asks, as sweetly as ever.

I rest my head against the window. Shove my hands into my armpits since I can't hide them in my sleeves.

"There's nothing to talk about."

I know. I know it's the least convincing lie I've ever told. I know they recognize that they're watching me fall apart right in front of them and that I should talk to them. I can't go through my entire life with this secret locked behind my teeth and expect to survive it.

But I can't do it now.

I think, maybe, when we get back to campus, I'll finally be able to cry. I can feel it building up behind my eyes, stinging in my nose. I hold it in for now and hope I can get it back later, when I'm alone. These three have seen enough tonight. They don't need to see my tears too.

Max is turning onto the main road along the lakeshore right back to campus when a police siren chirps and the telltale blue and red lights flash from an unmarked car parked along the side of the road. Like it's been waiting for us.

"Dammit, Nat," Max says under his breath.

I'm too far gone to feel any of the shame or fear or guilt I know should be pummeling me as Max pulls over onto the small shoulder and the cop drives up behind us.

"What happened?" Tasha asks. Their voice shakes with their nerves. "You weren't even speeding."

Max doesn't answer, because they're going to figure it out in a matter of minutes.

The cop takes his time walking up to Max's door, shining a flashlight through the windows to make note of each of us before asking for the registration and all of our licenses.

Max gives me a look as he reaches across me to get the registration from the glove box, lips pinched and seething disappointment in his eyes. Celeste and Tasha pass their licenses to him, but when he holds a hand out to me, I have nothing to give him.

"I still don't have a license."

Max scoffs, and the cop says, "School ID?"

"I left my wallet at home."

The cop crouches down and shines his flashlight right in my face, getting a good look at me as I squint and hold up a hand to shield my eyes. He takes out a notebook and pen. "Date of birth, Mr. Conti?"

I wince, sinking lower in my seat. I try not to mumble as I tell him my birthday. Cops don't like mumbling. I even add a respectable *sir* at the end.

He scribbles it in his notebook and tells us to sit tight while he runs our information. Like it's even necessary when he knew me by sight.

The car is quiet for a moment after he's gone. I tuck my chin to my chest and hide my face behind a hand like it will shield me when Celeste inevitably says, "What did you drag us into?"

Max shakes his head, gripping the steering wheel so hard, his knuckles go white. "Grand theft auto is a new one to add to our records, huh?"

I drag my hand down my face as Celeste and Tasha, understandably, lose their shit. I only hear it in bits and pieces, and I feel nothing. I deserve their rage, just like I'll deserve it if they decide to cut me out of their lives after this. I deserve every bad thing that's coming to me.

But they don't deserve any of this.

The cop returns after a few minutes. "I'm going to need you all to step out of the vehicle, one at a time. Starting with you, Mr. Palazzola." He pronounces it almost like *calzone*. Missing the second *a* and the *t* sound of the double *z*. My brain homes in on that and it takes me too long to realize what's happening.

"He didn't do anything," I say. The apathy that's blanketed me is the only thing that keeps it from coming out as a desperate cry. "I'm the one who took the car."

"I am very aware of that, Mr. Conti, but he is driving a vehicle that was reported stolen, so he has some questions to answer."

"And what about them?" I jab a thumb toward the back seat. "They didn't do anything either."

"And they'll still have questions to answer. This is what happens when you make your friends accessory to your crimes."

I'm not 100 percent sure if he actually says that last part, or if it's my conscience manifesting vocally.

Max gets out of the car with his hands clearly visible, and then it's my turn. I come around the front of the Jeep, hands up until the cop has me turn around and put them behind my back.

"Do you have any weapons on you?" he asks as he snaps cuffs onto my wrists. It's not unfamiliar, but it has been a while since I've been in this position and I can't say I missed it.

"No." My pocketknife was taken from me years ago, and my parents were vigilant in keeping sharp objects away from me after I broke my wrist.

He doesn't cuff Celeste and Tasha. A tiny bit of relief manages to punch through the numbness, and I breathe out a grateful sigh.

They're going to be traumatized enough because of this. Because of me.

They don't need to add being handcuffed to it.

CHAPTER 31

I FEEL LIKE I'M sixteen again, sitting in a holding cell with Max, the silence between us stretching past the point of reconciliation. This has to be the last straw.

Max wanted to be friends again because he assumed I must have changed since high school, and now that I've proven that I really, really haven't, he'll be done with me.

The cops didn't bring in Celeste or Tasha, at least. Max and I sat together in the back of the cruiser while the officer asked them his questions until backup came to ask them some more and take them back to campus while the two of us were brought into the station.

I confessed to my crime readily enough. Anything to get Max out of here without another strike against him.

And because these cops don't know me personally, they take my eagerness to come clean as an invitation to parent me or something.

They start with a kindhearted appeal to my senses, like:

"You have such a bright future ahead of you. You're a

college freshman—you have so much potential. You should be focusing on school, getting your life in order."

And when that gets no reaction, they move on to shaming me.

"Is this the kind of person you want to be? Really? Stealing from family?"

Because, go figure, that Jeep belongs to Aunt Francesca.

When I still give them nothing, the cops try out their well-practiced intimidation tactics.

"You're eighteen now. If your aunt decides to press charges, you could see time for this. Your age can't protect you from consequences anymore. Keep this up, and you'll spend the best years of your life behind bars."

I keep my head down through it all, tugging at my sleeves that won't budge and scrubbing at a coffee ring stained into the table in front of me. One of the officers mutters something about lost causes and I honestly don't get why they even care. They wouldn't give me this much grace if I were anything other than a dumb white kid.

It's going to take a couple hours for our parents to get here.

God. Max's dad is coming to get him. He's going to find out he's been hanging out with me again and then Max is going to suffer for my actions just like he always does.

Or maybe Mr. Palazzola will decide to finally cut the rot out at its source.

I'd let him. Anything to keep Max safe.

Max sits in the far corner of the holding cell, one leg drawn up with an arm draped over his knee. He stares at the wall directly across from him, picking at his nails and chewing on his bottom lip like he's actually going to tear the skin off.

I should apologize.

If this is it, the least I can do is tell him I'm sorry.

Maybe if I don't, he'll be less likely to give me another chance. He really shouldn't be giving me any more chances.

I lie down on the bench on my side of the cell, knees curled to my chest. I stay like that for a minute or two before stretching out onto my back, hands folded on my chest, letting my eyes lose focus, gazing emptily up at the ceiling.

What would it be like, to simply stop existing? Not even to die. Just . . . fade out to nothing. Maybe I could drift so far out of my body, nothing ever pulls me back in. I'll put my body on autopilot, let it sustain itself however it needs to, but I'll play no part in any of it.

It sounds so freeing.

I think I'd like it.

But maybe I can't have it, because as soon as Max opens his mouth, I'm fully present, hyperaware.

"I'm sorry, Nat," he says, and I sit up so fast, I have to hold on to the bench with both hands so I don't fall right off.

"No," I say. "Stop doing that. Stop taking the blame and

saying you're sorry when I'm the one who keeps fucking everything up."

He shakes his head, this sad look on his face like he really does believe he has something to be sorry about.

"I knew you were in a bad place and I was still a dick to you."

"Max." I press my hands together in front of me, like a prayer. "I made you an accessory to grand theft auto. You were downright fuckin' civil compared to how you should've been."

He's still shaking his head, still chewing his lip, until he says, "I shouldn't have let you drive off campus. I knew it wasn't your car. I was just afraid to push you too hard, upset you too much."

"I'm not a fuckin' toddler, Max."

"No. But I know you've always got one foot off the ledge. I'm terrified that someday, you'll take the step."

I stare at him, unblinking as the meaning behind his words settles. All the shame I should have felt earlier crashes into me at once, like a wave pulling me under and slamming me into the rocks below the surface.

And I break against them.

The tears I've been trying to let out for ages finally gush out of me like a reservoir overfilled to the point of rupture. I can't hold in the audible sobbing and when I try, it bursts out all the more aggressively for it.

I fold into myself, hide behind my arms curled around my head so no one can see how deeply the anguish twists my face.

Max is afraid for me. Afraid to lose me. And he has every reason to be. I have spent too much time teetering on that ledge lately, and every passing moment has me tipping closer and closer to the drop-off.

I don't know how to pull myself back to safety.

I feel Max's footsteps more than I hear them. Quick thuds across the concrete that vibrate in the soles of my shoes. I feel him sit down heavily on the bench beside me. I still flinch when he touches my shoulder. His fingers shy away, but I chase the touch, turning in my seat to fling my arms around him and bury my face in his chest.

He holds me tightly against himself, one hand between my shoulder blades and the other on the back of my head. He presses his face into my hair, his breath hitching as he cries with me.

His voice cracks as he speaks. "I wish you'd told me about the wedding. I would've gone with you. You didn't have to face him alone, Nat."

It takes me a few choppy breaths before I manage to say, "How do you even know about him?"

"You told me."

"I did not."

"Yeah. I get why you wouldn't remember, though. It wasn't a good night."

He says it like it haunts him, and that's enough to spark the dull embers of a memory. Enough to get the idea of what happened.

Max caught me about to fall and when he pulled me back, I broke down and told him everything. He's always known. I didn't have to do all of this alone.

I don't have to do this alone anymore.

It's enough to slow the tears, to turn the dial down on the gasping sobs, leaving me with less frantic, hiccupping breaths. I don't move away from him yet, and he doesn't ease up his hold on me. I've never felt as safe as I do now, with Max shielding me like this.

"We'll get through this, okay?" he says, his thumb rubbing a soothing line along my spine. "But you should talk to someone about what happened to you. It can be me, if you want. But it should probably also be a therapist. Okay?"

I nod against him, twisting the back of his shirt in both hands. Holding on for dear life.

MAX'S DAD ARRIVES FIRST.

I'm hovering at the edge of sleep when the door swings in on loud, squealing hinges, jolting me to full consciousness with a thudding heart.

"You're good to go, Mr. Palazzola," the officer says. I jump to my feet as if this lady would let me follow Max out. She raises a hand to stop me. "Not you, Mr. Conti."

"But . . . but he—"

Max touches my elbow as he steps around me. "It'll be okay."

"But . . ." It's the only word left in my vocabulary.

He turns to look at me when he says, "I promise." And then he's gone.

It feels like the last time I'll ever see him. Like all those years ago, watching him walk down the hall at school, never looking back. His dad will make him transfer and that'll be it. I'll be alone again.

I stand in the middle of the cell, staring at the door with my hands hanging limply at my sides until it opens again and the same officer says, "Your turn. I hope you realize how lucky you're getting here, kid."

"I always get lucky," I mutter as I follow her out into the station.

Mom and Dad look exhausted, standing there with their shoulders slumped, eyes empty. They've taken the time to change out of their wedding clothes, Mom in leggings and an oversized cardigan, Dad in his Sunday sweats and an old Buffalo Bills sweatshirt from the nineties Super Bowl era. Mom's hair is piled on top of her head in a loose bun and it looks like she haphazardly wiped the makeup off her face, traces of mascara left under her eyes adding to the defeated look of them.

This is nothing new to them, picking me up from the police station.

The officer leaves me with them, and they spend a good minute silently looking at me. I can't meet their eyes. I stand with my shoulders around my ears, eyes locked on my shoes, hands fisted into the front of my shirt, and shame burning in my cheeks.

Dad moves first, turning for the door without ever saying a word, and Mom follows suit.

A black hole has opened in my chest, devouring every last lingering shred of hope or emotion left inside me.

My parents gave up on me a long time ago. This doesn't hurt. It can't hurt.

I trail after them, dragging my feet out into the parking lot, dimly lit by sconces flanking the double doors into the station. I don't realize something's wrong until Seth appears at my side. He takes my arm and pulls me to the left. I suck in a startled breath, almost tripping over myself as Seth moves me to stand half behind him.

I look over his shoulder just as Mr. Palazzola stops in front of Mom and Dad and starts yelling. Max stands several feet back, rocking up onto his toes like he's ready to jump in if things get out of hand.

"I am sick and tired of your piece of shit son getting mine

involved in his bullshit," Mr. Palazzola says, shouting, jabbing his finger in my direction, so close to Dad that he has to reach over his shoulder to do it. "If you're not going to discipline your child, I'd be happy to do it for you."

He looks at me then, eyes burning with hatred. If we weren't standing right outside a police station, I'm pretty sure he'd barrel right through Dad and Seth and come for my throat.

I wouldn't even try to defend myself.

Dad puts a hand up between them, not touching, but ready to push him back if he gets any closer. "Calm down, Tony. Max isn't even in any trouble."

"This time. What about next time? How far is your kid gonna take it next time?"

"Your kid is fully capable of making his own decisions."

Mr. Palazzola shakes his head, absolutely fuming. Seth's grip on my arm tightens.

"I'm taking this to Hartland," Mr. Palazzola says. "Right to the dean of students. They've got that Honor Code shit. They won't stand for this."

I watch the fight bleed out of both of my parents. The hand Dad held up in defense drops to his side as Mom's chin drops to her chest. They always knew I'd end up here. Always knew I'd snuff out every undeserved opportunity to better myself. College was never going to last. The only place on this planet that I will ever fit into is a prison cell.

A pair of cops comes outside, drawn out by the shouting, and Seth uses the moment of distraction to tuck me safely into the back seat of Dad's car, climbing in after me.

I keep my head down. I can't bring myself to look out the window and see Max again.

I think Seth asks me if I'm okay, but I can't find the energy or the will to respond. He doesn't ask again.

It feels like hours before Mom and Dad get in the car. Mom gives a soft, despondent sigh and Dad reaches across the center console to hold her hand in her lap.

"Where did we go wrong?" he says quietly, and Mom only shakes her head. He takes a moment to gather himself before starting the engine and leaving the police station behind.

They still don't say anything to me, because there's nothing left to say. They've tried it all before, and nothing has ever changed.

I never changed.

I know it wasn't always like this, even if I can't remember a time when it was different. I know, because there was no reason for it to be like this before. There are framed photos in the house of the four of us smiling, Mom and Dad holding me just as tightly as they did Seth.

But so much has happened since then, so many years have passed, it might as well have been another life. All those good memories have been razed by trauma.

Because that's what it was.

Trauma.

I have lived through a traumatic experience and it changed everything and now I want my life back. I want my family back.

Max is right. I have to talk about it.

Halfway home, I finally find it in myself to answer Seth's question.

"I'm not okay."

It comes out raspy, broken.

All three of them look at me, Mom and Seth turning to face me and Dad looking into the rearview mirror.

I meet Mom's eyes, and the skeptical look in them stings.

"We need to talk about your brother."

CHAPTER 32

IT'S HARDER TO SAY than if I were confessing to murder. Like I'm the one who did something wrong.

But when I finally manage to choke out the words . . .

It's like I've spent my whole life suffocating and I'm finally taking my first full breath.

Even if they don't believe me, even if they think it's another one of my games, I've said it. It's no longer lodged there between my ribs, festering.

They don't immediately react. The world continues to speed by in a blur, the low rumbling sound of the pavement passing beneath us filling the silence in the car.

If they don't believe me, I'll find somewhere else to live during school breaks. If Mr. Palazzola gets me kicked out of school, I'll get a job. A tiny studio apartment. And I'll manage.

I've just pushed through the most difficult task I've ever been faced with. Everything that comes next will be easy in comparison.

I'll be okay.

But then Mom's face crumples. She gasps out a sob, and I notice the way Dad's knuckles have whitened on the steering wheel, the clench of his jaw.

"Why didn't you tell us?" he says through his teeth.

He's furious, but it feels different from the fury I've seen in him before. It doesn't feel directed at me.

"You didn't ask the right questions," I say.

Mom's weeping gains a pitch, and I watch a tendon jump in Dad's jaw. He mutters a low "Fuck."

Seth sniffles to my left. I thought I had cried myself out with Max, but it builds up again now, and by the time we make it back home, I'm exhausted and dehydrated by all the tears. No one makes a move to get out of the car once it's parked. No one knows how to handle this.

I have the most practice dealing with it, so I guess I'll show them how it's done.

I unbuckle my seat belt and step out of the car without ceremony, dragging my feet toward the front door.

Mom scrambles out after me, Seth and Dad following more slowly.

"Nathaniel." Mom's voice is still thick with emotion. She stands in the beam of the headlights, one hand held up by her chest like she wants to reach out to me, but it's been so long she's unsure of the motion.

I offer her half of a joyless smile. "All those times you asked me what was wrong with me? That was it."

I barely make it to my bunk before I crash, and I wake up in the dark hours later to the sound of Mom shouting somewhere in the house. I can't tell what she's saying at first, her words nothing more than a rush of fury.

But then I make out my uncle's name, and everything sharpens.

"We all defended you!" Mom is screaming. "I don't care how old you were, you sick fuck! You ruined him. You ruined my family. You better hope I never see you again because I swear to god . . ."

My pulse races, knowing who is on the other side of that phone call. But I've never heard Mom's anger used in my defense. I feel myself exhaling, despite the horrible night I've had, and it lasts until I fall back to sleep.

In the morning, I find Mom and Dad at the kitchen table with their hands wrapped around steaming mugs of coffee, looking like they didn't sleep at all last night. Mom's crying again as soon as she looks at me. I stand there at the end of the table, holding on to my elbows and staring at the floor.

"What do you want to do?" Mom asks after a moment of quiet sobbing.

I blink up at her, brow furrowed. I glance over at Dad, and he watches me with that same simmering fury behind his eyes.

"What do you mean?" I say.

"Do you want to go to the police?" Dad says gruffly.

It's the last thing I expect him to say, what with my history with the law, the years that have passed, the inaction they took when Aunt Rosa tried to press charges for Gianna. I thought Mom's shouted threats at him would be the end of it, and honestly, that was enough for me.

But it's kind of nice that they see the law as an option. That they're willing to tear down Mom's little brother for me. I just wish they'd been willing to do it for their niece.

I shake my head. "I . . . no. It won't do anything. I just want it to stop affecting me so much. I think I should, like . . . go to therapy. And I want to go back to school, but Mr. Palazzola . . ."

"I'm calling him in a little bit," Dad says. "If I can't talk sense into him, I'll go right to the school."

I lower my eyes, a flush of shame heating my face. I don't think he needs sense talked into him at all. He's right. I'm a bad influence and I've broken the Hartland Honor Code and it's a miracle I'm not in jail right now.

"And I'll look for therapists that specialize in this," Mom adds. "We'll get you whatever help you need."

I blink through a sudden surge of tears, and before I realize they're moving, Mom's holding me against her, arms squeezed tightly around my waist, and Dad's hand is resting on my shoulder. It should feel awkward, uncomfortable after all the resentment between us, but I'm so starved for their

affection at this point that I melt into it. It doesn't fix anything. Not even close. It'll take a lot of time and a whole lot
of effort to earn back each other's trust, I know.

But the black hole in my chest coughs up a little sliver of
hope.

I rest my chin on top of Mom's head as she hugs me. Sniff
back my tears. "I think . . . I think I want to talk to cousin
Gianna too. But I've never been able to find her online."

Mom pulls away, her hands staying on either side of my
waist, and she sighs softly, almost like she was expecting it
but was hoping it wouldn't come up. She brushes my hair
out of my eyes and gives me a sad smile.

"I'll call your Auntie Rosa. I owe my sister an apology
anyway."

GIANNA ANSWERS ON THE first ring, like she was waiting
for my call.

"Hey, Nate."

The last time I saw her, we were both nine years old.
We shared a matchbox car collection and she joined mine
and Seth's epic sword fights in the woods behind Nonna's
house. She was the only one in our whole family who called
me Nate. I hated it and she knew it, so I would make fun of

her high-pitched, whiny voice, because she hated it and I knew it.

Her voice is deeper now. A little husky. She's probably a great singer.

"Hey, G."

She stays quiet. She must know why I'm calling. I'm sure Aunt Rosa warned her I was about to bring up her trauma. So I guess there's no point in dragging my feet about it.

"I, um ... ," I start. I've put myself through this conversation so many times over the years. Everything I'd say and all her possible reactions. Staged the whole thing out in my head. But now that it's happening, I don't know how to say it. I take a deep breath. "You know the thing with Uncle—"

Her sigh stops me short. "You too, huh?" Her voice is thick with sympathy.

My knees go out from under me slowly, and I sink to the floor beside the bunk bed. She must've known as soon as Aunt Rosa brought it up. Why else would I want to talk about it?

"Yeah." It comes out as a strained whisper. I close a hand loosely around my throat as it tightens with threatened tears, feel the vibrations of my words as I continue. "I'm sorry I let the family turn on you like that. I should've said something. I shouldn't've made you go through that alone. I'm so sorry."

She doesn't answer right away. Her breathing is deep and

steady. I close my eyes and move my hand off my throat to grab a fistful of my hair.

"We were kids, Nathaniel," she says quietly. "And it was scary. With the way our aunts reacted . . . I doubt I would've said anything either, if you'd come forward first. They didn't exactly make it safe to speak up. And, well . . . I didn't even mean to come forward myself, really. I didn't understand that what was happening was wrong. I told my mom like I was telling her about some kind of game, and her reaction is how I realized it wasn't."

My hand tightens in my hair, the pull on my scalp keeping me grounded. "I didn't understand either."

She sighs again, soft and sad. "We were just kids."

CHAPTER 33

TWO DAYS LATER, I get an email from the dean of students informing me of my disciplinary hearing scheduled for when campus reopens after break. Academic dishonesty and questions of character have been raised by members of the Hartland community.

This would've happened even without Mr. Palazzola's prompting, with the cheating on that test and all. But he didn't help.

Gianna and I have been texting since I called her on Sunday, catching up on each other's lives for the past nine years and reminiscing on the fun we had together as kids. We don't talk any more about our mutual trauma, but we both know it's an option if we need someone who understands what we've been through.

I'm in a much better place than I was, she'd told me on our call. *It took a lot of therapy and a lot of time, but things don't feel so dire all the time anymore.*

I don't think I've ever felt this hopeful in my life. It's almost scary. Like I don't know who I am without my head filled up with darkness, and once it's cleared up, I'll have to get to know myself all over again.

I message Mickey to ask if he ever feels like that too. Afraid to get better because you won't know yourself anymore.

Mickey
I used to. But I like who I'm becoming.

Even Seth has started messaging me here and there since he and Riley went back to base Sunday morning, but I haven't heard from Max, or Celeste, or Tasha. I don't even know if Max's dad let him go back to school that night.

Mom and Dad drive me back to campus early Monday morning. Things are still mostly quiet and awkward between us, but that edge of animosity is gone. I can finally breathe around them.

"You sure we can't come with you?" Mom asks as I climb out of the car outside my dorm.

"Just me and the honor committee," I say. Mom and Dad have planned for lunch in town and a walk on the lakeshore while I'm in the hearing, sticking around in case I end up expelled and we have to pack up my room and take me home for good. My heart lurches at the thought of it. I never thought college would be for me, but I like Hartland.

I might even love it.

"You'll be all right," Dad says, and I realize I'm frowning, staring at the dashboard in front of Mom. I blink a few times, getting my head back on straight before looking at Dad. "Just be honest and show them you're committed to doing better."

I nod, swallowing against the anxiety closing my throat. "I will. I am."

They smile at me before driving off. They haven't smiled at me in so long.

I take out my phone as I head across campus, sending a group message to Max, Celeste, and Tasha with shaking hands.

> You guys free?
> I get it if you don't want to hear it
> but if it's ok I want to apologize
> to you all in person.
> I have an honor code hearing in 20 min.
> Gonna wait outside the office till then
> if you have time to meet me there.
> I understand if you'd rather cut contact.
> I'm sorry.

I check my phone every couple of steps on the five-minute walk, but no messages come through.

It's okay. It's fine. I don't blame them for wanting a clean break. It's not like Celeste and Tasha even knew me for all that long and I never gave them much of a reason to want to keep me around after almost getting them arrested.

If the committee lets me stay, I'll keep my head down the rest of the semester. Make sure I ace all my finals. Next year, I'll show up on campus a brand-new person, ready to make new friends and treat them the way I should've been treating my old ones all along.

I will learn my lesson.

But when I step into the hallway where the honor committee office is, Celeste and Tasha are sitting on a bench outside the door, Max pacing in front of them.

I stop short.

They're waiting for me. And they look nervous.

Max sees me first, almost tripping over his own feet when he turns in his circuit and locks eyes with me. Celeste and Tasha jump up from the bench and the three of them converge on me so quickly, for a split second, I'm sure they're about to beat me down.

But then Tasha hugs me, Celeste smiles, and Max says, "We thought they called you in already."

I shake my head, hugging Tasha back loosely, afraid that if I hold on too tight, they'll dissolve like sand in my arms. "Long walk across campus," I say.

Tasha steps back but keeps a hand on my arm. They look like they've been crying, on the verge of tears even now.

"We were worried about you," Celeste says. Her voice is sincere. Not a hint of gossip or curiosity.

I breathe out an incredulous laugh. "Worried about me? After what I did?"

The three of them exchange glances before Tasha says, "We knew you . . ." They take a second, wet their lips, and try again. "We knew you weren't doing okay that night. We're not going to hold it against you."

"But it's also not going to happen again," Celeste adds. There's no heat behind her words. Just the truth.

This is my second—and final—chance.

I shake my head, looking at the floor between our feet. "It won't. I promise. And I'm sorry. So fucking sorry."

My voice gets caught in my throat, and then my breath hitches, and before I know it, I'm on the bench between Tasha and Celeste, Max kneeling in front of me as Tasha pets my hair and I tearfully tell them the truth.

Not the details. They don't need to know every sad, horrible thing. But enough.

Something bad happened to me as a kid and the shame and the guilt ate me up until I didn't recognize what was left. I acted outrageously because I wanted someone to notice and built up a shell of apathy because I wanted so badly to not care what other people thought of me.

But I do care.

I want people to look at me and see someone they can count on. Someone they can trust. The surface stuff doesn't matter so much.

In the end, I say, "I still don't know who I am or who I'm going to be, or how long it'll take me to figure it out."

Tasha runs their fingers gently through my hair, almost soothing enough to quell some of the anxiety sparking in my chest. "We already told you," they say. "We'll stick around while you figure it out."

"Unless it turns out you're actually a huge piece of shit," Celeste adds, but she bumps me with her shoulder, her smile small but affectionate.

I blink back a fresh buildup of tears. "I'll do my best not to be that again." I look at Max as I say it. A promise to him more than anyone. His eyes crinkle in that smiling way of his, and he gives me the barest of nods.

He understands me completely.

TALKING TO THE HONOR committee feels like I'm just making flimsy excuse after flimsy excuse for my behavior.

My mental health was suffering, and it impacted my ability to concentrate and study, and I resorted to cheating.

I had something of a mental breakdown and stole my aunt's car to come back here, back home.

"I know that my mental health struggles don't justify my actions," I say. "That's why I'm committed to working on my health and how I manage my bad days so nothing like this happens again. My parents are arranging for me to see a therapist, and I have a good support system here on campus, in my friends. I don't want to hurt other people just because I'm hurting. Ever again."

Professor Loren was obligated by the Honor Code itself to report my violation, but he defends me to the committee itself. "Nathaniel's work has always been authentic up until this point. He's shown great care in his research and writing, and I have seen his potential." He purses his lips and gives me a lingering look that I can't return. "I can't speak on his behavior outside of my classroom, but I would hate to see that potential go to waste."

My hands are in my lap under the table, so they can't see the way I wring them together as they discuss the plan of action right in front of me.

They're leaning in too close together, speaking too quietly for me to hear, and it's absolute torture. I can tell by their faces who wants to give me another chance and who would rather personally kick my ass right down to the lakeshore, and the split is way too close for comfort.

I close my eyes and take a slow, deep breath, try to embody some of Max's unending optimism.

Someone clears their throat, and I open my eyes to find the committee with their eyes on me again.

"Well, Mr. Conti," the dean of students says. "I don't need to remind you how seriously we take the Honor Code here at Hartland."

I wipe my sweating palms on my pants and shake my head. There's a whole ceremony at the start of the year where the freshmen come up one by one to sign their names in an old book. You can't graduate without signing.

He sighs. "But we also understand that things happen, and poor decisions can be made during times of great stress. This is your first transgression as a Hartland student, so we are willing to move forward with disciplinary probation. However, based on your history prior to enrollment, and the concern with involving this campus in a serious crime, you will not be given the same leeway as your peers. If you misstep again, we will bypass suspension and move forward with expulsion, without refund of tuition and fees. As a part of this probation, you will meet biweekly with your academic advisor, and monthly with a counselor in our medical center. Do you understand?"

There's that feeling again. That light flutter of hope, like the black hole is shrinking further, giving back more of myself with each breath.

"Yes." I breathe the word more than I speak it. "Thank you." I look at Professor Loren. "Thank you."

He smiles and nods, and when they dismiss me from the room, my friends are waiting in the hallway to close around me in celebration.

CHAPTER 34

TASHA MASSAGES BLEACH INTO the left side of my hair. If there's one thing about myself that I'm 100 percent sure of, it's my look. I could have kissed Tasha when they offered to fix my hair for me.

All four of us are in their room, Styrofoam containers of fried food from the Throne Room spread out on the floor between the beds. I have a half-eaten pizza log in one hand and my phone in the other, and I am—for once—legitimately happy.

"Are you writing a whole freaking thesis on your phone?" Celeste says when she looks up from her laptop and catches sight of my thumb swiping feverishly across the screen. "Damn."

"Nah. Just a whole freaking speech outline." I shove the rest of the pizza log in my mouth and wipe my hand on my pants so I can go at my phone with both thumbs.

I stepped out of the judiciary hearing feeling inspired. I meant it when I said I was committed to doing better.

Professor Huang might not accept my extremely late work, but I still want to do it.

Call it my own self-therapy before I get into the real thing.

I don't write about the trauma itself. Instead, I find myself writing about Hartland. About this semester in particular, and the people I met, how they've made me face down my own flaws and come out the other side wanting to be better.

The semester isn't over yet, but I already know that it's going to serve as a turning point. Down the line, I'll be able to look back on how completely these few months changed my life, and that suits the assignment just fine.

I'm still working on it as we all pile onto Tasha's bed, my hair covered by a shower cap while the bleach sets, a TV show I pay no attention to playing on their laptop. Four people on a twin-sized bed is already a tight fit, but Max is close enough that he might as well be on me, one long leg stretched under mine, which are bent at the knees, his chin on my shoulder to get a better view of the screen.

If he reads over my shoulder as I type, that's okay. Maybe it'll help him understand just how valuable he is to me.

He's been pretty quiet since I came out of that office. He went with me to tell my parents the good news and see them off, answering all their questions about what he's been up to these past two years, but he's barely spoken since then. The way he keeps looking at me, I know he's saving whatever he wants to say for when we're alone. So when it's time to wash out the bleach, I motion for him to follow me into the bathroom.

There's a big stall with a tub tucked behind the door. I run the water lukewarm and push my sleeves to my elbows as I kneel beside the tub to duck my head under the faucet. Max sits on the edge, waiting, and watches intently as I scrub a towel through my hair after.

The intensity makes me nervous. I give a bit of an awkward chuckle. "What's the look for?"

He bites his lip, still looking at me like he's seeing past my skin and bone and into my freaking soul. "Just trying to figure out if you're really as okay as you seem."

I scrunch a handful of wet hair in the towel, looking back at him quietly as I take a moment to really think about it myself. I feel good right now, yeah. I know it's not going to be easy or quick, reaching a place where I feel like this more often than not, but I know the steps I have to take, and I'm ready and willing to take them.

So.

"I am. Really. You were right, about talking to someone." I take another moment to arrange my words the way I want to say them, wiping away rivulets of water soaking into the collar of my sweater. The towel is big enough that it hides most of my arms as I dry myself, but I'm not hiding anymore. Max already knows what's been under my sleeves all this time. It's okay if he sees now.

"I told my parents," I say. "Getting the words out was almost impossible. Felt like I was choking on them. But once I said it . . . god. I could finally breathe."

Max's eyes go soft, the corners of his mouth pushing up into the smallest smile. "They believed you?"

I nod. "Didn't even question it. Almost felt like they were expecting some kind of shoe to drop eventually."

He's still smiling, even as his eyes water and he reaches toward my wrist, fingers hovering until I give him a small nod. He takes my wrist gently and pulls it toward him, stretching my forearm out between us. He ghosts the fingers of his other hand over the ridges of scar tissue there. I keep my eyes on his face.

I don't think I've ever felt so fragile but safe at the same time.

"I'm proud of you, Nat," he says.

I have to look away then, watching my free hand fiddle with the towel pooled in my lap. I huff an unconvincing laugh. "For what?"

"Surviving."

I smile. Yeah. I'm proud of me too.

EPILOGUE

EYES CLOSED, I TIP my head back, the warmth of the sun on my face a stark contrast to the icy water engulfing me from the waist down. A shutter clicks.

A soaked white costume shirt is nearly translucent against my skin, the sleeves rolled neatly to halfway up my forearms. The spray of the small waterfall tucked into the woods on campus collects on my face faster than the sun can dry it.

The water is cold enough that it wrenched my breath right out of my chest when I first stepped into the creek. I was all prepared to dive right in without testing the temperature first. Probably would've sucked in a lungful of water at the shock of it if Tasha hadn't stopped me.

"Not all art has to be suffering," they'd said with a hand on my elbow.

Now, they snap a few quick shots as I push my dripping hair off my forehead with both hands, droplets falling like rain into the stream around me.

"Just a few more," they call out over the dull roar of the waterfall. "You'll start going blue soon."

I shake my hair out, let it fall back into my face. With my fingertips grazing the surface of the water at my sides, I tuck my chin and give the camera my best smolder, even as my teeth chatter with the way I shiver.

Tasha's been inundated with requests to sell prints of their work lately, and they want to launch their online shop with new photos to post alongside some already popular ones.

I'm not their only subject, of course. Celeste and Max stand behind them, Celeste in her knight costume and Max in dirty, torn burlap, swinging my prop swords at each other.

When we finished our *Sir Celeste Steps on Sleazy Bard Nathaniel* shoot and Tasha asked me to pose for some serious shots, it made me feel valuable. People like Tasha's photos of me enough to pay for them.

I know the credit is all on Tasha, but it still feels nice. And maybe, if things go really well, we'll both be able to make some kind of career out of this. Even if not, I like posing for them. I like that I can be someone else in front of the camera and as soon as it's off me, I can step out of that role. Like a little break from the search for myself, but never enough to lose sight of it.

Tasha takes one last photo as I dip down to my chest in the water and wade forward, eyes on theirs behind the camera.

They're blushing as they lower it. "Okay, please get out before you get hypothermia."

The blush stirs up a thought I've been mulling over on and off for days now. I can't meet their eyes again as I step onto the shore and they meet me with a fluffy towel that they wrap around me, rubbing their hands on my arms to help warm me.

They frown, bottom lip jutting out in a bit of a pout. "Ugh, I'm sorry, Nathaniel. This could've waited a couple weeks. If you get sick, I'll never forgive myself."

"I'll drink a gallon of chicken soup tonight, just for you." I reach out with the towel wrapped around my hand to wipe away a few stray water droplets from their arm. "It was good to do this now. Now you can focus on lacrosse."

They smile, grabbing a corner of the towel to scrub against my hair. "You'll be there, right?"

"Of course."

Their team made it to NCAA quarterfinals, and I'm tagging along with Max and Mickey to cheer them on.

"Max and I are making signs," I add.

They bounce on their toes, eyes widening. "Witch hat?"

I grin down at them. "Witch hat."

They do this cute little wiggly dance as they kneel down to pack away their gear, and I pull the towel tight around me as I watch Celeste pretend to beat Max down with a sword. Even with that playing out in front of me, I can't stop myself from glancing over at Tasha every few seconds.

I'm pretty positive they're still into me, even if I've given them plenty of reasons not to be. And I like them too. I could ask them out.

But they deserve stability, and I know I can't give that to them. Not yet.

This is the back-and-forth I keep having with myself. We like each other, and if I don't do something about it now, I might miss my chance. But if I do, and I'm not ready, it'll only end up hurting us both.

I don't want to hurt them, and I don't want to hurt anymore.

After I get some more therapy under my belt, when I feel more steady in myself. I've only had one session so far, with a medical center counselor. I'll give myself the summer, seeing the therapist my parents are sending me to and fixing my relationship with my family, and if I'm ready when we come back for sophomore year, and Tasha is still interested, then I'll ask.

For now, I'm more than happy to be their model and friend.

Once I feel dry and warm enough, I gather up the purple silk cloak of Sleazy Bard Nathaniel and clasp it around my shoulders. Tasha zips their camera bag and looks up at me, squinting against the sun.

"We should get you inside."

I motion toward Celeste and Max, the collection of

swords they're not using laid out in the grass. "We could ambush them?"

Tasha grins wickedly, nodding, and we creep over to silently take up arms, let out battle cries as we descend on Celeste and Max.

An epic sword fight in the woods of Hartland University.

Tonight, I'm having dinner with Mickey James and his friends while mine are at practice. Jaysen wants me to teach him how to juggle playing cards. Tomorrow, I'm having a video call with Mom, Dad, and Seth—a thing we're going to try to do weekly from here on out. After that, I'll meet Max, Tasha, and Celeste in our library loft to study.

It's all so simple, but it feels revolutionary.

Breathless with laughter, foam sword in hand, I tilt my face toward the sunlight filtering through the canopy, and close my eyes with a smile.

ACKNOWLEDGMENTS

SOPHOMORE NOVELS ARE NOTORIOUSLY painful to write. *In Repair* was especially difficult for me, as I wrote it during a time when my depression had reached its deepest, darkest point, and on top of that, this story picked at old trauma I had mistakenly thought long healed. So I first need to thank my doctor for giving me the tools to survive that time, and my husband, Rushtin, for supporting me through it.

Thank you to my editor, Kortney Nash, for taking me and this story on, and for being so patient with me and the ages it took me to write it. I really thought I was turning in unreadable trash that first round, but your enthusiasm and editorial eye brought me to love this book. For something as close to my heart as Nat's story, I *needed* to love it the way you made me do so. Thank you.

My agent, Jennifer Azantian, thank you as always for being the best advocate I could ask for. I'm certainly not the easiest to work with in my tendency to hide away, but you still make me feel so important. Thank you as well to Brent Taylor for your work with foreign rights.

Thank you, Samira Iravani, for the absolutely stunning design, and thank you, Jessie Mahon, for your gorgeous art. When I first saw the initial black-and-white sketch of Nathaniel, I remember thinking, *That's him. That's Nathaniel, exactly as I see him in my head.* And when I heard about the plans for the color duality, I knew the team really understood the story. I couldn't ask for a better outward representation of my words.

Rachel Murray, you may not have worked on *In Repair* with me, but you were the one who approved it and let me run with something deeply personal and difficult to talk about, and for that I thank you. Thank you as well to Laura Godwin, Lelia Mander, Alexei Esikoff, Allene Cassagnol, and the rest of the team at Macmillan, Henry Holt Books for Young Readers, and Godwin Books, for your hard work and support.

Thank you to my family—my parents, and my sisters Samantha, Marissa, and Deanna—for being my biggest fans and most fervent supporters. I know this one won't be easy for you all to read, but just know that Nat's feelings toward his family have nothing to do with my feelings toward you. I love you all.

And to my best friends in the world, Vivi, Kaze, Grace, and Low, thank you for existing. You make every day more bearable.